THRONES FOR THE INNOCENT

Wings Press, Inc.

C. W. KESTING

Thrones For The Innocent

"You know because you share," he began. "You have also lost, haven't you?" He reached for Alex's hand, took a firm grasp of her first three fingers and squeezed.

"The pain never leaves. I can see it in the lines of your face." He sighed. "Mothers never let go."

Alex's heart froze in mid-stroke before restarting with a silent bang. She wanted to pull away, to shake her head in defiance, cast off this street loon and rub away the hopeful lies.

But she couldn't.

The truth poured from this man's dark eyes like a hemorrhaging dam, flooding the shallow valley of Alex's emaciated soul. The silence between them lasted only the briefest of seconds, yet screamed through Alex's head like a high-pitched Forth of July rocket. Then a word popped into her head that fully described the emotion she felt flowing from his gaze.

Communion.

The frail man held Alex captive in a claustrophobic cocoon of prophetic anticipation for a moment longer before speaking again.

"It doesn't have to end with your Cora Rose." He smiled warmly, yet with a stern countenance and then continued, "In fact, it shouldn't."

Alex stared in disbelief, torn between terrified revulsion and mystical curiosity.

He couldn't possibly know about Cora. What's going on here?

"There is something you can do," the man suggested, his eyes pleading, still moist. "You can still take action."

The man closed his eyes and sighed; his face sunken and drawn with exhaustion. When he reopened them, his eyes were cold and commanding, nearly void of color.

Those eyes terrified Alex; yet she peered into them as if through a rip in time, unable to resist their firm gaze.

"You must find a way into the Crease," the man whispered. "Find *yourself* there, and learn from the Devices."

What They Are Saying About Thrones For The Innocent

Thrones For The Innocent, by C.W. Kesting, delivers a tale filled with the intensity of loss, guilt and sorrow. The journey to hope and redemption—with all the mind twists and ethereal turns—is surprising and satisfying. A great paranormal read!

*lizzie starr
~*Prince of Dark Ness*

Kesting has written a heart-wrenching story of love, despair and rebirth with descriptions so vivid as to make one think they were real and not on the page...a flowing tale that interweaves the real and the paranormal while exploring the balance of the universe. He writes with a multi-faceted style: at once simple, but powerful in both the narration and the description of the bleakness of a lost child...yet ethereal when discussing the mystical complexities of the soul.

~Katherine Petersen;
SF Site reviews

Every parent's nightmare will become a special purgatory for you in this supernatural tale of guilt, grief, and redemption. Kesting does not tug at your strings, he yanks them, grabbing both heart and breath as he pulls you into and through a story - and a dimension - that is simply all too real to ignore. His powerful descriptions and dialog, talents he establish, in his first novel, *Rubicon Harvest*, take a quantum leap forward as Thrones for the Innocent grips you, shakes you, and leaves you nearly senseless at the end - but yearning for more.

~G. David Clark,
Sunset Dancer
Yorrik's Lot

Other Works from the Pen of
C. W. KESTING

Rubicon Harvest:

Jon Webb, an ex-soldier framed for murder, evades capture in an attempt to both clear his name and save his family from covert scientific experimentation. Detective Sal Gionetti races the clock and wrestles corporate conspiracy to unravel the truth behind the mysterious homicide, but his efforts uncover an intricate technological plot that threatens to alter the course of human evolution.

THRONES FOR THE INNOCENT

C. W. KESTING

A Wings ePress, Inc.
Paranormal Novel

Wings ePress, Inc.

Edited by: Elizabeth Struble
Copy Edited by: Sara Olds
Senior Editor: Elizabeth Struble
Managing Editor: Leslie Hodges
Executive Editor: Marilyn Kapp
Cover Artist: Richard Stroud

All rights reserved

Wings ePress Books
http://www.wings-press.com

ISBN 978-1-59705-620-5

Published In the United States Of America

Wings ePress Inc.
3000 N. Rock Road
Newton, KS 67114

Dedication

For my own guardian angels—my two treasures: Ryan and Aeryn.
May they never loose their way.

*"It's a poor sort of memory
that only works backwards."*

—The White Queen to Alice
from *Through the Looking-Glass*
by Lewis Carroll

Lusus Naturae

Oh, that little bitch!

As he gave chase, he caught fleeting glimpses of her between the skeletal trees—a flash of purple sweater, twitching blonde pony-tail, faded blue jeans—crashing desperately through the wooded maze.

She was fast, but he was closing.

Angry branches snapped and lashed at his face as he pounded through the forest. He stumbled and nearly fell as he sidestepped through a narrow break in the twist of maples and oaks. The terrain here was sandy and a spread of thick roots had knuckled their way through the loose ground. The land sloped away from his house, sweeping toward the paved nature trail that eventually led to the park. The huge back yard had been engineered for natural run-off and gradually dropped away from the elevated deck that hung off the back of the house. From the railing it was at least an eight-foot drop to the thick manicured lawn—apparently not much of a challenge for a determined eight-year-old.

Willful, troublesome bitch!

He could hear her ragged breathing as she ran across the inclined forest floor. His own breath whistled in his throat, tight from the unexpected exertion. He pressed further into the wooded acres, his long adult-sized strides overmatching her frantic scamper.

He also knew her asthma was beginning to awaken, squeezing her chest and freezing her lungs. He heard her as she struggled with each tight breath: Pant. Wheeze. Pant. Wheeze. He patted the reassuring bulge of the inhaler in his front pants pocket.

Increasing his pace, he gambled and selected risky paths through low shrubs and over tangled deadfall in effort to catch her before she reached the trail and then the park. His legs pumped high and hard, feet crunching and crashing through the carpet of dead sticks and dry leaves. Low branches slapped and scratched at his face as he bulled his way forward. A crooked finger from a young maple snagged his eye-patch and partially ripped it from his head, tearing a fine bloody line across his cheek.

"Shit!" he exclaimed.

She made the mistake of turning her head at the sound of his voice, lost her balance and bounced off a thick knobby oak. She staggered, but did not fall.

He closed within a few strides, the eye-patch swinging from his ear by a strand of frayed cloth. They faced one another for a single, empty moment. Her eyes bulged with terror; her face was flush with red panic as she sucked air into her shrinking lungs—each breath rapid and erratic.

Pant. Wheeze. *Pant. Wheeze.*

She pushed off the gnarled trunk and ran harder, her arms swinging wildly as she threw herself carelessly down the gentle grade, bouncing clumsily off the trees.

He sprinted after her, bounding past the last of the large oaks. The woods thinned as the trail materialized from the bottom of the hill, snaking out of the surrounding cover. He quickly scanned the length of the wide walkway to its visible limits; first north, then south. Deserted now, but that didn't mean that at any moment someone wouldn't come coasting in from either direction on bike or skates.

He had a sudden inspiration and with a great gulp of air he shouted:

"Hey!"

Out of pure conditioning for obedience she stopped and turned toward the adult voice. Her face was a mask of desperate exhaustion; her shoulders were stooped and rocked with laborious breathing.

Pant. Wheeze.

He paused in the chase, held up the light blue albuterol inhaler pinched between his fingers and shook it gently, taunting her with the promise of rescue medication. Her eyes locked on the little plastic dispenser and for a long breathless second she appeared to consider surrender. He snatched the dangling eye-patch from his ear, stuffed it in his back pocket and smiled in anticipation.

A suffocating moment passed between them; the only sound on the hill the strained whispers of her asthmatic lungs. He finally heaved a sigh, swallowed hard and snickered while shaking his head. She stifled a weak scream and then abruptly turned and bolted down the remainder of the gentle slope, out of the tree line and into the gulley that bordered the trail.

She dropped like she'd been shot, falling headfirst into the shallow ditch. A few tense seconds passed as he watched for her to rise. In the time it took for him to slow his own respirations, two clouds crept in front of the sun, dragging their shadows across the woods.

When she didn't get up, he pocketed the inhaler and ambled down the hill toward the spot where she tripped. Stepping carefully over the thick tangle of briar and scrub at the rim of the gulley, he reached down at one point to retrieve her sneaker from a particularly dense patch of overgrowth. He gazed again down the ribbon of paved trail in both directions.

Deserted.

Stepping to the edge, he peered into the ditch. She lay nearly motionless at the bottom, curled on her side, wheezing severely between weakened sobs.

"Poor thing," he cooed. He reached into his front pants pocket and withdrew an inhaler; this particular one yellow and white and held more than just albuterol. He shook it with one hand, mixing the aerosolized medication, while he rubbed at the raw, scratched skin just below his dead eye.

"Let's get you back home."

One
Cardboard Angels

The day, like her mood, was gray and deflated; and as dawn broke over an apathetic city she stood in the frigid winter garden, staring at the memorial.

Silver frost and grainy snow textured the bottom half of the bronze plate, partially obliterating the lower two-thirds of the inscription, leaving only the first line visible:

Into Your arms, O' Lord, the wandering child

Like an ice bath, those eight words chilled her core so completely she was convinced any breath at all would mist about her head in the same ghostly veil as this morning, regardless if it were in the dry, crisp cold of November or the broiling humidity of deep August.

She refused to think of the line as an epitaph, though any other description truly fell short. Regardless of its intent, the phrase—meant more as an appeal than prayer—was not an original. Lifted from the rambling, albeit well-intentioned text of the anonymous pastor's memorial service, it was the only utterance from that blurry day that Alex could even vaguely remember.

Besides, David, a devout and practiced believer, had said he liked it. So, after an insipid and feckless discussion they had eventually agreed, and like some twisted proclamation that simple phrase was forever etched into the metal plaque.

She stood reluctantly, if not reverently, at arms length from the memorial, gazing at the twelve-inch square of frozen bronze embedded in the limestone wall. Only the first few letters of the name were visible above the crusted margin of icy snow, mocking her with false hope and teasing her with unrealistic possibilities. That partially hidden name reflected the painful truth back onto her empty heart and she shivered, more against the chilling memories than the bitter outside temperatures.

She suddenly felt the urge to do something, anything, to alter her sense of loss, to tip the scales of weighted fate back in her favor and bring balance to her miserable existence. Stepping forward, feet crunching in the crisp fresh snow, she pulled one fuzzy mitten off with her teeth. She reached out with her bare hand and brushed the brittle crust of snow from the plate. Her fingers traced the grooved lines of the entire engraved message:

"Into Your arms, O' Lord, the wandering child."
Cora Leigh Rose Age 5
Missing: May 30, 2007

Squeezing her eyes tight, she wished the innocent wish of a child—that the mere act of clearing and revealing her name was somehow magical enough to bring the little girl home; like rubbing an enchanted totem or whispering a special incantation under one's breath was certain to repel all species of Boogie Men from the shadows beneath the bed.

Her fingertips grew numb against the icy bronze and it wasn't until she felt the tears on her eyelashes begin to freeze that she finally released a long-held breath in a shuddering foggy sigh and fell to her knees. She leaned into the wall with both arms straight, her head bowed between, her straight dark hair spilling out from beneath a handmade knit cap.

Tears fell into the soft carpet of snow, melting small irregular holes in the otherwise unbroken surface. Her shoulders hitched uncontrollably with torturous sobs.

Alexandra D'Meiter knelt in the small wintry courtyard of Saint Peter's school and wept for her daughter until she felt dehydrated. After nearly three years, the painful void at the core of her heart had not completely healed. The emotional scar tissue responsible for that sort of amelioration had never formed.

Perhaps that was in part due to her reluctance to move on without fully knowing the truth about her daughter's disappearance. The terrifying uncertainty of whether or not Cora was even alive only paled in comparison to the horrifying speculations Alex had about the little girl's disposition if she was.

She partially—and selfishly—blamed Cora's father for her inability to let go. The memorial plate had been his idea, in an effort to both honor and—more to the point, she felt— symbolically bury her little girl. It made it easier for him to continue on. It brought closure; and to a surgeon that was, ironically, important. It meant that he could confidently move on to the next part of his life, much like moving on to the next surgery, the next patient.

Of course, a new posting as chief of surgery and fresh new residents every six months or so had certainly helped him focus on other things besides his lost daughter. Or on Alex, for that matter. There was no lack of distraction—or closure—in Dr. David Rose's life.

Alex stopped herself mid-rant, angry and ashamed by her bitter and petty jealousy. She shook her head and rubbed her wet eyes with a nappy mitten, sniffing at the moisture gathered at the tip of her nose as she rose to her feet.

David was a good man and meant well. She was always unfair to him it seemed, and even though he could never know her inner most thoughts—and thus, understand her completely—she still felt guilty and embarrassed for her immaturity. He was an easy, if not convenient, scapegoat.

She simply despised the memorial in principle. Despite his noble intention, it still gave the impression of hopeless acceptance; and Alex refused to bury her daughter, symbolically or otherwise, without confirmation. The damn ornate bronze plate just reinforced David's resignation.

Mothers never let go.

She had heard that phrase somewhere, perhaps murmured in the crowded parlor during the memorial service (*Remembrance* service—she had to remind herself. That was what the pastor had called it) and it had stuck. She liked it; not merely for what it represented but more for how it captured the point completely. It was all-encompassing, laser accurate, dead-nuts on the money.

Mothers never *let go.*

And yet, here she was, in spite of herself—or, perhaps, in spite of David—staring at a frozen plaque with her daughter's name engraved on it.

The truth was, as pathetically heroic as it sounded coming from a hopeless cynic such as Alex; she came more in defiance of cruel Fate. Her daughter had to be *somewhere*. Alive or dead, she had to be somewhere. And whichever finality Fate had chosen for her, little Cora was more than likely alone and scared.

That's what both terrified and angered Alex the most. That, and the overwhelming burden of guilt.

She reached into her coat pocket and fished around for the small bag she brought with. Her car keys jangled as she knelt forward, pulled her hand free, and spilled the contents of the bag onto the stiff snow: a scattering of pastel Skittles candies and shelled pistachio's. The lighter, irregular nuts remained afloat on the surface of the snow-crust, yet the symmetrical hard-shelled fruit chews imbedded in the crunchy white. These had been Cora's favorite snack. A small paper-cupful at bedtime with a glass of water and a few chapters from a book had cemented their nighttime ritual into tradition.

Now, Alex pulled a tattered paperback from inside her thin parka and flipped it open to a marked page. She stood near the wall, one hand on the bronze plate, the other holding open the book as she began to read from one of the *Magic Tree House* stories. The serial books by Mary Pope Osborne were also Cora's favorite. Wonderfully researched and dramatically crafted, the tales of Jack and Annie, the time-traveling siblings, captured the imagination as they journeyed through the past, gathering clues and solving mysteries.

Alex read in a soft, clear voice with just the right amount of character inflection during the dialogue. It had been important to Cora that the story was read with attention to detail and concern for substance. Each character had a voice—a personality—and should be read as such. Even the narrative had to have an eloquent, impartial, and yet omniscient tone.

After two short chapters, Alex twisted her wrist and gazed reluctantly at her cheap watch—a child's timepiece featuring Dora the Explorer. According to Dora's hands, Alex was running late again. She frowned, sighed, and closed the book; sealing a blue satin bookmark snugly between the pages.

"I have to go, baby," she said sadly. "Don't want to be late on my last day." Alex winced against the threat of tears. Her breath plumed about her head in the crisp frigid air.

"I miss you, Princess Pea," she whispered. Her shoulders hitched and she bit her lower lip, but her resolve held.

She turned to walk back down the snowy path through the courtyard when a voice stopped her. She looked up, startled, realizing a tall figure stood a few feet from her.

"Lexie." The man greeted her softly.

She swallowed a cry of surprise, suddenly embarrassed—ashamed of her open vulnerability, her emotional weakness, her past mistakes, and her disheveled appearance. Her cheeks warmed with the sudden flush of emotions has she plunged one hand into the deep pocket of her cheap powder-blue parka, hiding from his sight the ill-fitting dingy pink mitten. In her other hand, clad in mismatched fuzzy yellow, she held the book.

"David", she murmured. Her embarrassment slowly shifted to irrational and defensive anger, as she watched him gently fold his arms.

His long cashmere overcoat hung tightly around his square frame, the tails fluttered around his legs in the stiff breeze. His perfectly pleated charcoal slacks fell straight to dark, expensive leather shoes that seemed to defy the winter elements.

His light blond hair feathered across his brow with a small gust of wind and he brushed the lock back with a casual sweep of a leather-gloved hand. The gloves alone, she was certain, cost at least three times what her second-hand, coffee-stained coat went for brand new.

Her anger swelled, though now focused inward at her own feminine weaknesses. As usual, he looked incredible and she hated herself immediately for allowing the impulsive attraction.

Damn him.

"You look good, Lex," he said. Both his smile and his eyes sparkled.

Damn him.

The worst was that she knew he meant it. Every word. If David was anything, it was sincere. The genuine article. The real deal.

Christ, she thought. *Just go over a give him a hug.*

Instead, she shrugged off the compliment and pouted her lips defiantly. She rolled her shoulders in a ridiculous attempt to appear regal in her ripped and frayed undersized parka, purple knit cap, and mismatched mittens.

He nodded placid acceptance. With a few gentle blinks of his soft green eyes and an understanding, compassionate sigh, he strode forward. He stopped short—a comfortable distance—and offered both arms in such a way that she would have the choice of embrace or two-handed shake.

She opted for the shake, cursing both her stubbornness and his easy diplomacy.

"Which one is that?" He nodded toward the book in her hand. Her breath caught in her throat momentarily and she feared that she might break down right there, collapse into his strong arms and sob until she had nothing left. A tiny, yet powerful part of her desperately yearned for exactly that and the temptation was naggingly strong.

But she understood temptation now and refused to bow to its will.

"Number eighteen," she answered softly. "*Buffalo before Breakfast.*"

He nodded. "Hmm. The White Buffalo legend of the Sioux. I always liked that one."

Alexandra smiled politely; thought of a cutting retort but then let it slide.

The silence between them used to swell and fester until the actual surrounding air pressure seemed affected; but just recently the quiet pauses had become temperate.

There had been a time when Alex obsessed about those awkward moments. Days prior to meeting with David, she would lie awake at night speculating on possible scenarios, planning and rehearsing responses, plotting and practicing body language and various gestures; all in effort to get it just right. And that would be in preparation for the scheduled meetings. She would nearly die from anxiety when confronted with a surprise encounter.

But now, she was cool. She had it together, thank you very much. She was squared away and dialed in. She—.

"I'm sorry if I surprised you earlier." He motioned casually toward the entrance of the courtyard, interrupting her subconscious *I'm-all-right-without-you-as-I'm-sure-you-can-see* mantra.

Damn him, again.

"No," she answered softly. "I was just leaving. Got to get to work." She shrugged and stepped to move past him. He politely, gently extended an arm to stay her. She snapped her head up in what she meant to be angry defiance, but her tight face melted when she saw his sullen eyes.

"Please, Lexie," he asked. "Just a minute or two."

She softened her gaze, allowing him to continue. David was the only one who called her Lexie. In fact, she had always hated the shortened moniker; until he had whispered it in her ear the first time they slept together.

Damn him.

But damn me even more.

The pain in his face further weakened her stubborn resolve. David smiled weakly, sighing as he spoke.

"I know that you'll be leaving soon," he began.

Alex blinked a few times and then dropped her gaze. She had meant to phone him once she was on the road, to avoid just this type of farewell. Her lips quivered as she tried to form a response.

"It's okay," he added gently, sparing her the pathetic attempt at an excuse—another one of his many graces. "Elaine told me today's your last day."

Ah, Elaine, Alex thought bitterly. The department of surgery's own gossip monger. What she didn't already know, she could soon find out.

Could she be the new, and evidently improved, Mrs. David Rose, MD? Although that would be technically incorrect, as David and Alex had never been married.

If that were the case, then Elaine would be David's first wife; and David, Elaine's third doctor. But then, as quickly as she entertained that unfair assumption, Alex very much doubted that David would ever go there. She knew David was a better man than that—falling for a surgeon groupie like Elaine.

Still, Alex began to simmer and brood as he continued.

"I wanted to say goodbye, because I knew that you wouldn't." His voice remained sincere, even sad; but his eyes shimmered with the hidden truth.

Coward, those deep green eyes silently accused.

She narrowed her own gaze in defense, and then frowned with reluctance. She couldn't deny the reality and that pissed her off miserably. She felt tears threatening to spill.

David spared her once again by taking her hands in his and squeezing. A warm hood of compassion eclipsed the stern look in his face. He smiled and held her gaze. She felt herself melting in his presence and again fought the primal urge to fold into his large arms.

"I know you feel that you need this. To get away," he said.

She stiffened in anticipation of his disapproval, bracing for another condescending lecture—one of his few faults.

"Though I'm sure it's for all the wrong reasons initially, I have to admit that it might be just what you need." He was looking over her head now, vague and distant.

"We'll miss you," he added softly. She knew he meant the spirit of their daughter and not the entire department of surgery. She appreciated the sentiment and accepted it at face value, but still bristled at his pointedly barbed endorsement of her decision to leave Chicago for the decidedly rural environs of northern Michigan.

Before she could respond, he abruptly changed tack. He dropped his head and again caught her gaze with his aquamarine eyes, now intense and insistent.

"How are you doing, Lexie?" His voice was suddenly strong, with the demanding clinical tone of a physician prying facts from a difficult patient. The question, though simple and direct, was in fact severely complex—thickly layered and probing.

What had been actually implied was: *Are you still clean and sober? Has your work suffered? Are you taking your meds? Are you going to meetings? Are you seeing anyone?*

Alex closed her eyes and sighed. She hesitated and actually contemplated addressing all of David's unspoken concerns with sharp sarcasm, but then reconsidered. He truly had her welfare at heart, though it still burned her to have to admit her weakness and the subsequent undoing that resulted from its manifestation.

So instead, she took the high road: "I'm fine, David." She offered a tired yet confident smile.

He nodded, a glimmer of doubt flashed across his face before fading to acceptance. Their eyes locked and the familiar tension returned, weighing the moment between them with reluctant remembrances of the past.

David's eyes narrowed, and for a brief second—a quick lapse, really—Alex thought she saw the last of the anger and blame being pushed back, supplanted by suffuse forgiveness. She hoped that were the case, but was quick to remind herself of the dangers in wishful thinking.

He finally broke the tense silence, "So, Michigan, huh?"

She blinked a few times, resetting her social veneer, and responded, "Yeah. North Central. It's a nice little rural stop along 131."

David nodded, contemplating his next question.

"I don't plan on returning, Dave." She meant for the statement to have strength and conviction, but instead it came across desperate—almost defensive.

He continued nodding, sadly, yet unsurprised. "You'll stay in touch, I hope." The request was more searching than hopeful, bringing a glimmer of moisture to his eyes as he spoke.

She sighed and chewed the inside of her cheek, her eyes darted from sky to snow covered path. In time, her gaze reluctantly settled upon his chiseled Roman features as she shrugged.

"We'll see, Dave."

The sternness of his tight frown set hard lines into his face. He knew that meant *probably not*. She knew it as well, but was too much of a coward to admit it. She struggled with most of the twelve steps in her recovery program and the whole 'honesty with oneself' tenet was really kicking her ass. She hated feeling like this—the guilt associated with her inability to mete out complete and total honesty with every social exchange.

She was painfully certain that *normal* folks—those lucky enough *not* to have been cursed with the destructive weakness of addiction—didn't feel compelled to wrestle with uncompromising honesty on a daily basis. It wasn't expected from them like it was from the wretched and recovering alcoholic. Unless, of course, they were hard-line Catholics. Alex had been raised by both, yet had followed only one path ardently.

My cross to bear, I suppose, she thought bitterly.

They both opened their mouths to speak and with a patient smile David gestured for Alex to continue. She allowed the hint of a genuine smile to touch the corners of her mouth and her lips warmed from the flush.

"I really have to go, David. I'm already late."

He nodded, closed his eyes for a moment, and then stepped aside, offering the path to her. She slowly stepped past, just catching a whiff of his subtle cologne. The urge to leap into his arms flooded her chest with temptation bordering on insistent craving. She resisted the pull and strode down the snowy path.

She surprised herself as she stopped and glanced back at him over her shoulder. David was watching her leave; his wet eyes and aching expression made him seem small and fragile. Her heart melted and her stomach flipped in compassionate somersaults. She formed the words to say good-bye but her throat spasmed and all that she could muster was a pathetic squeak.

He raised his hand in a tired wave and spoke for them both.

"I am so sorry." He sniffed, blinked, and exhaled in a shudder. "I love you, Lexie."

She ground her teeth against the emotions and spun on her heels as the tears erupted. She quickly, clumsily, staggered down the winding path toward her car.

"I love you, too, David," she mumbled to herself. Ashamed, confused and in emotional agony, she faded into the breezy snow dusted woods.

Two

Cold steel chilled his back as he leaned against the rusty, filth encrusted dumpster; the layers of thread-bare rags that served as make-shift outer garments barely insulated his gaunt body against the wet winter evening. He crouched in an uncomfortable catcher's stance, frequently shifting his weight from left leg to right and then back, rocking on his haunches while trying to remain hidden behind the bulk of the overflowing metal box.

He risked an occasional glance around the dented corner of the container, yet the door to the apartment remained closed and the alley empty.

Squatting in the shadows of the frigid alley, he rubbed the cold from his exposed arms and massaged the aching cramps in his strained leg muscles. Ankle deep in the fetid black slush puddled against the crumbling brick wall, he flexed his toes against the numbing wetness.

Urgency had brought him here nearly four hours ago, beckoning, that was mellow and vague at first, but then pressed at him with a warm insistence he could not ignore. It had called to him in his sleep, a natural harmonious push, luring him from fitful dreams as he shivered beneath the cardboard blankets comprising his bed in another faraway alley. Yet, despite the exotic and euphoric pressure there seemed to be no hope of personal reward in the calling, no promise of self-fulfillment for heeding this alarm. He instead followed the ethereal impulse out of primal instinct—a nagging sense of rightness, an innate and selfless obligation to unconditional and uncompromising duty.

And when he awoke, he hadn't felt entirely himself. Literally, he felt as if someone—an other—had eased into his mind.

As the strength of this particular urge swelled, the importance of obeying the Other's emphatic will eventually consumed him; much as a tide washes ashore, progressively smoothing more and more sand with each rhythmic ebb and flow.

Now, at proverbial high tide, the enticing influence of this presence had his mind humming. The magnetic energy that led him to this rotten-smelling alley whined at full-throttle, a sense of near-completeness vibrated in his chest. Disturbing and graphic images—foreign memories, really—began to solidify in his mind, unwanted yet insistent in their detail.

In the span of one brief moment, his purpose was suddenly clarified, the instruction complete; and with this realization his body assumed a global sense of lightness. His heart quickened with the anticipation of necessary engagement, his senses sharpened with the flux of cause and effect.

He was suddenly *needed,* and someone or something depended on him. The Other—this oracle—had shown him this and subsequently brought him here.

A brisk wind spiraled down the narrow alley, twisting paper debris from the heaping piles of garbage in chaotic clusters. A wave of frigid air swelled above the dumpster, absorbing the rancid, oily stench as it passed. The current of air swirled about his head, carrying a mélange of ripe odors thick enough to be actual vapors.

The usually enticing promise of edible treasures in that spoiled fog became less meaningful to him, replaced by an acuteness that transfixed his whole attention on the battered metal door of the apartment across the alley.

He sighed heavily, his breath plumed in frozen gray tendrils about his dirt-encrusted head. He ran a shaky hand across his roughened face; grimy fingers tracing the dry furrows of his brow, the deep arid ridges of his cheek and the lines around his eyes. He caught his reflection in the cracked basement window of the building immediately behind him. A long scab infested and stubbled face stared back at him—a visage of homelessness. Yet the cast of his gaze was majestic and confident—his dark blue irises contrasted against clear vibrant white and sparkled with an ancient knowledge and wisdom.

His mouth, usually framed by chapped and bleeding lips and caked at the corners, now glistened moist with the renewed warmth of blood and eagerness. Hunger painted his face vibrant and pink—a hunger quite different from the intestinal cramping and growling that he usually wrestled to sleep each night as he bedded down in alleys or abandoned cars. This was a relic appetite, with a primitive, ancestral flavor. There was a justifiable presence behind it that seemed to perceive the man beyond the derelict days and homeless nights.

This energy was ageless, exhilarating, and frightfully alien; yet, at the same time, comfortably familiar.

Across the alley, the door to the apartment jerked against the frozen jamb once, then twice, finally swinging outward in a creaky rush. The interior of the room behind the door was dark. A shadow peeled from the darkness and crept into the fading silvery light of the alley. A woman stumbled awkwardly across the threshold, carrying a hastily bundled blanket clutched tightly to her narrow breast.

She plodded through the misty grey alley, the veil of dusk drawing long dim shadows down the cinder block walls. Splashing through shiny black puddles, wide-eyed and crooked at the waist, she shuffled toward the dumpster. Her clumsy gait caused her to trip and stumble, nearly loosing her balance as she struggled to maintain her grip on the wrapped bundle.

The commotion startled a squadron of pigeons rooting in the trash, sending them flapping toward the gauzy light of the low winter ceiling in a snapping beat of wings and gentle spray of feathers. A few of the dingy white plumes drifted across the watcher's face, and he resisted the urge to sneeze or rub his chill-bit nose against the tickle of the fine fuzz.

He watched the woman with the bundle turn her head in the direction of the scattered birds, tracking their ascent with twitching intensity. Then she feverishly scanned the alley; her head swiveled in hitches and jerks as if the mechanism of her neck joint had rusted—oxidized from the wet winter chill. Her pale, gnarled hands worked nervously at the messily bundled blanket, kneading the frayed and worn material between discolored fingers.

When she raised the lumpy blanket over the rim of the dumpster, a sudden gust of frigid air blew discarded food wrappers into her face. Startled, she gasped and dropped the bundle onto the rotting mound of garbage.

Concealed in the shadows, waiting for something—some force—to nudge him into action, he watched the woman swipe frantically at her face, trying to remove the sticky wax paper that clung from her chin. She succeeded in peeling the yellowed film from her face just as a startled mewling sound emanated from the interior of the dumpster.

The terrified innocence of that crying triggered some implanted instinct that was not inherently his, and without warning, surprising himself with sudden agility and speed, he lunged at the woman.

There was a flash of metal—a subdued obsidian finish—as he withdrew the pistol from his tattered rags. He leapt, thrusting forward from behind the shadows of the dumpster, firing round after round into the woman's midsection.

Four silenced bullets found their mark before the inertia of his attack forced him into, then in a tangle, over the woman. The alley echoed with the muffled shots, filtering out the distant calls of the rattled pigeons and the constant drip of melting ice in drain spouts.

As he strained to keep from falling onto his victim, he again heard the shrill keening from the dumpster. The high pitched cry tugged mournfully at ancient emotions and faded memories far removed from this time, tickling the fabric of some repressed past and stirring the potency of the presence—the Other—now within him.

Dropping the gun, he fell forward and fire exploded in his own belly. The intensity of the blaze burned from navel to spine in a slow, steady pulse. He broke his fall with outspread arms, placing him atop the woman, supported in push-up position. He glanced down between their bodies and saw the glint of a wide blade, disappearing from the hilt into the mess of rags he wore as a coat.

Dark, thick blood oozed down the flat steel, running over the white-knuckled claws of the woman's hands and staining the black composite handle of a hunting knife. The blood pooled between them in a slow surge. Now stabbed and still straddling her, his arms locked, their noses nearly touching, he stared into the eyes of the woman beneath him. Those eyes—rheumy and blood-shot, held his gaze without blinking.

A moment—perhaps a lifetime—passed, and in that frame of frozen time, the two strangers silently understood the essence of one another. The consciousness of the Other throbbed behind his eyes, pulsing in sync with the woman's rapid heart; matching the bounces in the hollow of her neck, beat for insane beat.

In the instantaneous vacuum that followed, a sudden crystalline awareness cut into him; and from the fringe of somewhere—*everywhere*—vivid, lucid memories of who and what this Other was flashed across the blank screen of his inner eye:

He was Eric McBride. Twenty-five and hopelessly autistic, a middle school dropout at thirteen and brother to two younger (and "normal") sisters. Sometimes he was not as smart as his sisters...

But there was that one time when he was smart enough to stay in the closet when the Animal came home...

That was where *Then* ended and *Now* began.

The powerful consciousness of the Other—this Eric—hummed now, again pressing into his mind, insisting its will, eclipsing his memory. In seconds the bittersweet melancholy of his lost life faded back into the chilling wet numbness of the alley. The pages of his past furled back into darkness; and in the time it took for two staggered breaths, he ceased being a homeless forsaken man and had become this Eric McBride.

And for the moment, his sorrow and self-pity was forgotten; a capacity for which he rarely enjoyed above the usual distractions of his addled mind.

With a grunt he pushed against the ground with one arm and the woman's shoulder with other. The knife pulled out of his thin belly with the effort, making a soft, juicy sucking sound. He rolled to one side and then clambered to his feet, grimacing and moaning in anguish. Blood sluiced between his fingers as he pressed the heel of his right hand against the wound.

The gut-shot woman remained on the ground, breathing rapidly, staring up at the darkening grey sky. A thickening pool of blood gelled around her, tendrils of the crimson spill swirled in the slushy puddles of snowmelt on the uneven concrete surface of the alley floor.

The crying from within the dumpster became weak and raspy, yet more desperate. Eric McBride, in the homeless man's body, stepped onto the raised lip at the base of the giant metal container and, once on his toes, reached into the ripe refuse with his left hand. He grimaced as he stretched into the filth, pulling the torn flesh of his belly wound, forcing fluid clots of frank blood from the slit. His right hand pushed at the tight skin there, holding the edges from tearing further.

There, between the slick dented wall of the container and the ragged slope of congealed grease, rotten vegetable matter, and shit of indistinguishable origin lay the tattered bundle of the blanket. Eric snagged the frayed hem of the thin fabric with two fingertips and dragged the parcel up the foul smelling mountain of garbage. The bundle began to unroll and he frantically scurried up the side of the dumpster pulling himself deeper into the trash. The stab wound screamed as he threw himself headfirst halfway across the edge of the dumpster. Reaching in with both hands, he caught the small pink package as it completely unrolled from the blanket. He hovered there for a moment, balanced on the rim, head down in the filth, torn and bleeding belly pressed against the metal, arms growing numb as he strained to cradle the rescued baby.

He swung his legs and rocked his upper body up and out of the container. The inertia carried him clear and he fell back onto the wet concrete with a splash and hollow thump. His back slapped the alley floor and his head bounced as he cried out in agony.

There he lay, cradling the screaming infant to his chest. Tears filled his eyes, but not from pain. He heard the calls of the pigeons as they circled above, spiraling down from the heights, silhouetted against the iron-gray sky.

He turned to look at the woman lying next to him. Blood bubbled from the corners of her mouth as she drew ragged breaths. Their eyes locked and a frozen beat of time passed before the nearly forgotten songs of the Crease began to hum again in Eric's head.

The images the songs brought were flashes of motion and sound, like clips from a movie run at dubbing speed. These pictures—the woman's memories—were violent and senseless, disturbing and blunt.

Eric saw the things that loving mothers and dedicated fathers dread even imagining. Things that brothers of slain sisters are loathe to revisit. He stared at the woman with a mix of vengeful fury and bewildered repulsion. The woman glared back, her eyes pleading with Eric in desperate agony.

Then, the moment flickered out and the images faded. The woman blinked, coughed a lump of blood from her throat and spat it weakly onto her chest. In a raspy voice, wet and gurgling, the woman finally spoke.

"How did you know?" she asked Eric, her eyes squinting in an effort to comprehend. She swallowed hard, grimacing against the pain in her blasted stomach.

"How could you have *possibly* known?" she repeated weakly.

Eric slowly closed his eyes, turned his face to the sky and allowed the last whispers of the Crease to caress his mind. He thought of his sisters and their innocence, and he solemnly wished for their forgiveness. He had failed them in their time of need; stupid and trapped in his broken mind he had cowered in the dark shadows while they had pleaded hopelessly for their lives.

He remained supine in the alley, hugging the hoarse baby to his chest, bleeding freely from his belly, and waited for merciful sleep to take him.

Three

"Anesthesia to Trauma One. Anesthesia, Trauma One." The overhead page echoed across the lofty ceilings of the operating room hallways. A moment later, as if triggered by the calm monotonous voice , the pager on Alex's hip vibrated.

She finished tapping the bubbles from the plastic syringe, recapped the needle and placed the assembly on a folded green towel on her cart. She fingered the recall button on her pager and glanced down at the message screen.

Silvery text marched across the luminescent green field: *Trauma 1. Stat. Ex Lap for GSW.*

She sighed and pushed her cart out of the workroom and into the hall. Nurses and technicians scurried past in a flurry of blue cotton scrubs, paper masks and colorful OR hats. She negotiated through the traffic and around a corner, pausing to allow a patient-filled gurney to pass.

The young woman on the gurney had her eyes closed, yet a peaceful smile touched her lips. Tight black curls spilled out from under the blue mesh hairnet. A stocky white-haired woman in a loud floral-print cover-up jacket pushed the head of the gurney with one hand while gently supporting the chin of the patient with the other. Her eyes lit with excitement as she passed Alex and her anesthesia cart.

"Hey, girl! Drinks tonight at O'Tooles?" she bellowed.

Alex smiled and shook her head as the image of tall frosty beer mugs flashed in her mind. The memory of the bitter, hoppy tang of a cold draught tickled her deeply, teasing for just a moment, as it always did.

"Can't. I'm on call," she explained.

"On your last day?" the older woman exclaimed. She was now past, looking back over her shoulder, still pushing her patient toward recovery.

Alex nodded and shrugged with a smile.

"Talk to Greenbaum and get him to switch with me—oh, no. That wouldn't do. Hell, have *him* pull your last call. He owes you, right?"

Alex shrugged again.

"What do you got?" the woman asked, nodding toward the trauma rooms.

"Exploratory laparotomy. Gun shot wound," Alex answered.

"Who's on for trauma?"

"Jamison." Alex frowned.

"Ugh!" The woman grimaced and shivered as if she had bitten into an overripe grapefruit and tasted onion instead.

Alex just smiled as she watched the woman push her gurney through the automatic doors and into the recovery room, then continued on her way to the trauma rooms, pushing her cart before her.

~ * ~

Trauma room One was an orgy of chaos with too many bodies in too small of a room. A cacophony of voices competed for dominance over the crashing of metal instruments on stainless steel, the incessant ping of monitor alarms and the whine of a charging defibrillator.

From one corner, a woman shouted out lab values in successive rapid fire, while from the center of the crowded action a young man's voice cracked as he yelled: "Clear! Everybody clear!" Without a pause, the buzzing hum of the defibrillator snapped as it discharged three-hundred joules of energy into the chest of the naked and supine body splayed on the table. The patient's arms and legs stiffened with the shock, the torso arched up and then flopped back down.

The scene wasn't uncommon to Alex and after six years of providing anesthesia, the confusion and mayhem of a trauma did nothing to startle her. In fact, if anything, it had the opposite effect.

The reality of a life circling the drain right before her eyes actually had a calming, energizing quality and she embraced it. While those around her spun and danced awry, she funneled her energy into one crystal clear mental algorithm that forced her into calm concise management of any situation. Where others thrashed and slapped at the turbulent waters of a crisis, she calmly treaded the surface.

"Sinus tach, people! Got a pulse?" a different voice announced—assertive, yet with a twist of whiny arrogance. "Good. Okay, pressure? We got PVC's now. Start a Lido drip. Airway? We need an airway—where the hell is anesthesia? I'll cut an airway if you can't get that tube, Ted!" Dr. Jamison's voice was caustic, excessively tense, and annoyingly feminine.

"I'm here!" Alex shouted firmly, "Anesthesia's here."

"Make a hole!" Jamison directed as he shoved students and residents aside.

Alex pushed through the crowd to the head of the table, pulling her cart behind. The corner of the steel cart caught Jamison on the hip and he grimaced with a curse.

"Shit! Why wasn't there an anesthesia cart already in here!" he demanded, rubbing his hip.

Alex glared at him for a fraction of a second then went to work assembling her laryngoscope blades and endotracheal tubes.

"Restocking, for one," she answered succinctly as she snapped a blade on to the handle and quickly checked the light.

"Preventing you from practicing anesthesia, for two." She flipped a plastic airway from a tray onto the table and grabbed the ambu bag from the resident that was mask-ventilating the patient.

"And preventing yet another unnecessary surgical airway because you botched the intubation, for three." Alex spoke calmly as she positioned the patient's head with her right hand, deftly slid the laryngoscope into their mouth with her left, lifted firmly and slid the tube through the vocal cords in one smooth motion.

She was out of the patient's mouth, connecting the breathing circuit and taping the tube in place before Jamison could respond.

"You may cut now, doctor." Alex turned the dial on the vaporizer, flipped on the ventilator and began tweaking the controls of the anesthesia machine. It was only then that she noticed the cavernous quiet that had fallen over the room. The only sound was the steady whoosh from the bellows of the blower and the rapid beep of the pulse-oximeter.

~ * ~

"Ted, finish closing. Staples and Telfa. Paper tape only. And be quick about it. We round at eight." Jamison stepped away from the table, crossed his arms, grabbed his blood-smeared paper gown at the elbows and snapped the ties in a single jerk. He shrugged out of the blue gown and rolled it into a tight ball. He absently tossed the wadded bundle in the general direction of a large-mouthed trash hopper and missed considerably, making no attempt to pick it up. He turned to face Alex as he tugged at the cuffs of his surgical gloves and snapped them off as one might shoot rubber bands from their finger. First the right, then the left glove shot straight into the tiled floor as he made no attempt to even aim at the trash. He never took his eyes off Alex, and she tried to busy herself and ignore his obvious glare.

He hovered at the threshold of the surgical suite, his hip holding the door open, impatient and nearly vibrating with adolescent rage. His relentless stare burned across the room.

Oh, fuck it. She finally conceded and met his icy stare with an ambivalent sigh.

Jamison craned his neck, jutted his jaw forward and pointed at her with a childish finger-gun as if he were some cocky playground bully. The gesture was meant to intimidate, but was instead tragically immature.

Alex batted her eyes innocently and then bowed with a flourish.

Jamison stormed out of the OR in an arrogant huff. The door swung silently closed after him.

"Asshole," she mumbled, hoping only to herself.

"No shit," Ted, the surgical resident, replied without looking up from his wound closure.

"Fucking-A," the scrub tech echoed.

"Amen, brothers and sisters," added the circulating nurse as she turned up the music.

~ * ~

"She's ready to be extubated," the nurse said, turning from the computer screen to greet Alex as she entered the unit. Alex sipped from a covered Styrofoam coffee cup, then set it down on the long wrap-around counter of the nurses station. She rubbed her eyes, yawned weakly and nodded.

"Been breathing on her own and fighting the tube for an hour. Last ABG was good and her tidal volumes are fine. God, Alex, you look like shit." The young nurse glanced at Alex only for the second it took to formulate that concise observation before completing her charting on the computer.

With a flourish of final key-strokes and the energy reserved for someone soon to be off shift, the young ICU nurse spun out of her chair and bounced to her feet, long ponytail swinging across her back as she moved gracefully toward the patient's room. She scooped up an armful of supplies from the counter as she passed.

Alex ambled behind the sprightly girl, wondering mournfully where her own youth and exuberance had gone. She knew the answer all too well and dismissed the dangerous and careless thought immediately before it could take seed and distract her already exhausted mind.

"Long night?" the nurse asked as Alex entered the darkened room behind her.

Moderately bright fluorescent lights flickered to life just above the head of the bed, eliciting a startled jump from the patient as her eyes adjusted to the sudden illumination. The ventilator's alarms went off in a series of beeps and steady mechanical cries as the woman in the bed coughed silently into the endotracheal tube, her chest rocked with the effort, her face reddened.

"Easy now, Kathleen. Easy. Anesthesia is here to remove that breathing tube. Just give us a second, okay," the nurse chided. As she opened up fresh suction tubing and an oxygen mask, she glanced at Alex expectantly, awaiting a response from her previous question.

"No more than usual, Mary. The last six hours always drag, you know." Alex answered softly.

"Yeah, I suppose," Mary agreed.

"So, your name's Kathleen?" Alex asked the patient as she leaned over and peeked at the controls of the ventilator. Nearly twelve hours earlier, in surgery, the frail looking woman was simply known Jane Doe Number One. Multiple gunshot wounds to the abdomen. Status post-cardiac arrest. A good save.

The patient nodded, again coughed silently into the ET-tube and screwed her eyes tight against the irritation.

"The police ID'd her from the open apartment leading into the alley where they found her," Mary added, as if Kathleen wasn't able to hear. Mary glanced at the patient and for just a moment, a sour look of revulsion passed across her face before she turned back to her work.

Alex disconnected the ventilator circuit from the breathing tube and silenced the alarms in mid-chirp with a practiced stab of her finger. Lights continued to flash across the panel of the machine, but the audible warnings were disabled.

A whisper of inhaled air, followed by the rush of exhalation echoed from the opened end of the tube protruding from the corner of the patient's mouth.

"Now, Kathleen," Alex began. "I'm going to un-tape this tube, ask you to take a deep breath in, hold it, and then blow out. Understand?"

The woman nodded and blinked rapidly to accentuate her willingness to be free of the endotracheal device. Alex nodded in response and smiled.

"Okay, deep breath. Good. Hold it. Now let it out." As she did, Alex deflated the balloon cuff on the end of the tube and smoothly slid it out with the exhaled sigh.

Kathleen coughed a few times then immediately began taking small gulps of air. Mary carefully suctioned the woman's mouth and then placed an oxygen facemask over her mouth and nose.

"I want you wear this for a little while, then we'll see how you do without," Mary explained. The patient closed her eyes, slowed her breathing and eased into a deep, even rhythm.

Alex removed her gloves and stepped to the sink to wash her hands as Mary brushed the used tube, tape and suction into the bedside trash.

"Thanks, Mare," she said.

"Not a problem." the nurse answered with a shrug. "Hey," she continued. "What happened in the OR between you and Jamison?" Mary's eyes were wide with the anticipation of gossip.

Alex dried her hands with a paper towel, then glancing at the patient first, responded with an arched brow and nonchalant shrug before whispering, "I refuse to fight any battles on my last day."

"Last day?" Mary was genuinely surprised, her face taut.

Alex nodded tiredly.

"Really." Mary's voice trailed off.

"Yep."

"Wow, I didn't realize it was that time already. So soon." Mary shook her head.

The two women left the room and Mary brushed the light switch on the way out, tossing a blanket of darkness over the patient; whose deep respirations purred within the thin plastic of the mask, fogging it's clear edges.

At the nurse's station, Mary propped her youthful hips against the tiled counter and considered Alex with a soft frown of sadness.

"I'll miss you. You were one of the better ones."

Alex smiled and nodded a thank you.

A brief but comfortable cushion of silence enveloped the two women. Then all hell broke loose.

Discordant alarms blared from the central monitors behind the low counter, shattering the full quiet of the post-midnight hours, filling the ten-bed unit with piercing tones.

The other three on-duty nurses popped from out of nowhere in immediate response, emerging from their own patient's darkened rooms—eyes searching for direction and explanation.

"It's mine!" Mary announced. "A run of v-tach in three." Then to Alex in a softer voice, "It's Kathleen." Her gaze swept back to the room they had just left.

As they both moved toward the room, the interior lights suddenly blazed to life. In the ghostly intensity of the over-the-bed spots, Kathleen sat bolt upright in the bed, as rigid as a corpse; the remote for the bed controls, room lights, and nurses call-light clutched in one tense hand. The death grip turned her hand bone-white; her fingers trembled from the force exerted.

"Kathleen?" Mary called out as they entered the room.

They circled the bed and Alex fluttered her gaze from the patient to the sharp blue-green spikes of the ECG tracing as it marched out the dangerously fast heart rhythm across the monitor above the bed.

"Kathleen, can you hear me?" Mary repeated.

"Two-forty? No way!" Alex exclaimed as she read the heart rate from the monitor.

"Maybe it's double-counting," offered a voice from the doorway. The other nurses had joined the scene in response to the excitement.

Alex quickly looked over her shoulder. The new nurse was just pulling a mask from her face as she opened the door wide enough to allow the crash cart to follow. Two other nurses guided the blue steel cart into the room and began opening drawers and popping caps off of vials.

"Let's get her down!" Alex commanded, intending to both lay the patient supine and immediately slow the lethal cadence of her heart.

As Mary reached for Kathleen, the patient's arm flew out from beneath the covers in a blur of bony paleness, her fingers spasmed into a crooked and severe claw, striking Mary solidly across the temple. The cold talons ripped deeply, drawing vivid blood from three distinct gouges.

The sheer force threw Mary aside and down, striking the other side of her head against the corner of the bedside table on her way to the floor. She laid still after the fall, crumpled on the gray tile, blood welling rapidly in the three troughs dug into the side of her head.

"Shit!" Alex blurted. One nurse leapt immediately to Mary's aid while the others joined Alex in approaching Kathleen.

Taken by surprise and unsure how to proceed, yet loathe to do nothing; Alex hesitated for the first time in a long time.

~ * ~

Eric McBride stumbled across the icy sidewalk, slammed his bony hip against a newspaper vending machine and nearly dropped the bundled infant. He shot out his other hand and stabilized himself between the machine and a light pole.

The bleeding from his belly seemed to have slowed, but wasn't completely staunched. With every erratic step warm rivulets of thick blood trickled down his abdomen, soaking the waistbands of his many layers.

The baby seemed to be crying much less, yet continued to work its mouth, searching weakly for nourishment. In addition to being hungry, Eric thought that its color was all wrong; pale like the flesh of a banana.

Not wanting himself or the child to remain exposed, Eric was forced out of the alley and remotely guided toward a new goal of steady red and white light. Calling to him from some place as far away as tomorrow yet also as near as yesterday, this survival instinct insisted itself upon him, cleared his cross-wired brain of distraction and pressed him into action and away from the incarnate evil he had left bleeding back in the alley hours ago.

Salvation could be found in the red and white light. The baby needed to be there. He needed to ensure that this happened.

So, with all of his remaining strength, he had struggled from alley floor and struck out toward that goal, cradling the infant in one arm while holding his slashed belly together with the other.

Now the lights throbbed up ahead, tall illuminated letters that blurred in his vision despite his attempts to blink them into focus. The sign seemed to float in the air: white block letters on a large red rectangle, blaring and bright. His destination seemed miles and miles from where he stood; yet he knew that he must get there whatever the cost.

He re-gathered what little reserve strength he had left, hugged the swaddled baby closer to his center of gravity and shuffled the last remaining block toward the emergency room entrance of Cook County Medical Center.

Sirens Doppler-shifted in the distance as snow began to fall.

~ * ~

Alex watched as Kathleen's face pulled into a stony grimace—not of pain, but of terror. Her eyes pushed the extreme limits of their tendons and musculature, threatening to burst from their sockets from some unseen pressure. Kathleen stared intently into a void only she perceived, and the emptiness revealed by her observation of that abyss reflected in the pale silvery cast of her eyes.

Suddenly, she turned toward Alex, slowly revolving her head in a single smooth motion. For the briefest of nauseating seconds, Alex was certain that the woman's head was going to spin about the axis of her neck a full three-hundred sixty degrees, ala The Exorcist.

"They know." The woman spoke, her voice calm and editorial. However, the expression on her face remained terrified, her body rigid.

"They already know, and now there's nothing to do but wait!" The words were spoken matter-of-factly and though they sounded as if they might be taken as an accusation, they were uttered without malice.

"They sent *him.*"

Alex licked her lips and quickly glanced at the monitor: *Two-hundred forty-five beats per minute. Impossible! Her heart will explode soon.*

"But now it's too late. Too late for reason. For excuses. Too late for apologies." The woman spoke clearly, without emotion. Her tone was that of quiet acceptance, which clashed dramatically with the horrified and twisted mask of her face. It was as if her mind was aware of a completely different reality than what her body was experiencing. Alex was afraid of precisely that. *If she didn't slow and control that heart rate...*

"My babies", the woman continued. A single tear clung to the corner of one eye. "I...I had to help them across. You see that don't you?" Her eyes remained unblinking, vacant and bulging. "They were born into sin and needed *me* to get them across." Kathleen swallowed, yet except for the muscles required for that task, her expression of terror remained unchanged.

"They needed me to save them. I tried to explain that to him." The tear finally ripened and crawled down Kathleen's cheek, tracing a thin ragged trail from the corner of one bulbous eye. Alex glimpsed the monitor:

Two-hundred sixty beats per minute!

Kathleen caught Alex's eye and held her gaze intently. There was depth and agony in those eyes; yet, also something else. A palpable presence, not altogether sad or even solemn, but rather smug. Even arrogant.

"What will you do, now that you know? Will you judge me for my actions? For saving my children from this sinful existence?" Kathleen asked, though Alex was no longer sure that Kathleen was actually doing the speaking. She cringed at that supposition even as the doubt formed in her mind, yet she couldn't shake the suspicion. Especially while looking into the fractured depth of those eyes.

Those eyes...

Two-hundred eighty! the monitor screamed; the green tracing now only a smear of color.

Kathleen swallowed with visible effort, and then spoke again.

"*I'll* look my fate dead in the eye. I'm ready for the Thrones."

A brief moment of stillness followed and then Kathleen simply fell backward into the mess of sheets on the bed and died with her eyes wide open. The molded grimace of terror on her face remained; an eternal death mask.

The ECG, abruptly flat-line, traced a perfectly straight green horizontal line across the grid. The steady tone of the monitor echoed dully within the still room.

~ * ~

As the X-ray tech pulled his portable machine from behind the curtain, Alex stepped aside to allow him an exit from the emergency department exam room. The young man closed the door behind him and Alex approached the gurney. An older nurse worked at dressing the wound on the side of Mary's head. Mary caught Alex's movement toward them and gave a weak sideways smile.

"Hey, Mare," Alex said. "How're you feeling?"

"Like a piñata," she answered, grimacing as the nurse re-taped the bandage.

Alex cleared her throat. "God, I am *so* sorry, Mary..."

"Alex, please, don't be. It goes with the territory."

The older nurse paused and leaned back slightly, pursed her lips and narrowed her eyes at Mary.

"Girl," she exclaimed, sounding like a lecturing grandmother. "They gets one chance down here. When they start to gettin' all belligerent and acting the fool with me, I tongue-lash them right back into the womb. And Lord Jesus help the son-a-bitch that raises a hand to me." The woman shook her head and sucked in her cheeks with defiant bravado.

Mary rolled her eyes and explained, "Ginny, this wasn't your typical Saturday night ER frequent flier. This was... I dunno..."

"Different," Alex finished.

Mary glanced at Alex and nodded slowly. "Yeah, different."

Ginny finished with the task of dressing the head wound and collected her supplies. "Well, whatever. You just can't let people get away with that kind of behavior—striking out at the one person trying to help you. Lord." And with that, Ginny exited the small private room, shaking her head.

Alex and Mary shared a glance and a smirk.

"So, what happened?" Mary finally asked. Her face creased with concerned. "All I remember is running back into her room shortly after we extubated her. Did she code?"

Alex shrugged.

"I don't know, Mare. One minute she was fine, the next she's in a kind of tachycardia like I've never seen before. Then she whacked you. Hard."

Mary's hand went to the side of her head and gently probed the bulky dressing. "No shit."

Alex hesitated, and then added, "She spoke. To me, I think. But it was weird..." She narrowed her eyes and recalled the calm words uttered by the dying woman. Mary lay recumbent in the gurney, her silence begging elaboration.

"Her voice was calm, almost serene. Wise. But her face was *terrified*. And her eyes, Mary..." Alex shivered unconsciously and instinctively hugged herself.

Mary nodded gently in empathy.

"Yeah, sometimes people go out in very bizarre ways. No one ever dies like in the movies." Mary counseled.

"No, this was different. There was something transpiring there," Alex explained. Her voice strained for confidence, seeking to believe in whatever it was she struggled to put into words.

"What did she say?" Mary asked.

Alex gazed uncertainly at Mary, almost ashamed, as if she were being asked to repeat some nearly impossible phenomenon for which she was the sole witness. This would most certainly be true if it weren't for the other three nurses present who could corroborate the tale.

"'They know'", she answered. "She said, 'They already know. And all there's to do is wait.'" Alex sighed and shook her head. "Then something about choices and regret. She said she was saving her children from sin." Alex shuddered.

Mary nodded. "Alex, It's not uncommon for people to express remorse and seek attrition at the moment they realize they're dying. If I had a dollar for every death-bed confession I've heard—"

"This wasn't like that. It wasn't desperate or even personal. It had the tone of an announcement. Revelational."

Mary offered an enigmatic smile and shifted her position.

Alex caught the look and immediately flushed. "Oh shit, I know what you're thinking."

"No, really, I'm not. Look, it was crazy and things happened fast, that's all."

"Yeah…"

"Besides," Mary added soberly. "If there really *is* a God, then that bitch is going straight to Hell."

Alex furrowed her brow, unsure of what the nurse meant.

"Alex, she killed her own kids."

Mary shrugged and elaborated with a sigh, "The cop who came in with her ID said they tossed her apartment and found three dead children. Ritualistic strangulations. Seven, four, and two years old." Mary's eyes turned violently moist, her voice cracked and she could only finish in a whisper. "How can you have faith in God with fucked-up people like that exercising their will?"

Alex stared into empty space, slack-jawed and shivering. Anger and sorrow suddenly squeezed her chest in a fearful embrace.

Killed her own kids?

Mary wiped her eyes with a trembling hand. "Well, someone must have found out and took matters into their own hands," she uttered weakly.

The door to the room suddenly opened with a professional double knock. A man leaned half in and addressed the room as an entity.

"Transportation," he introduced himself generically.

Mary frowned and tilted her head toward the door, explaining, "They want a head CT, just in case." She sniffed the emotion back.

Alex nodded, backing away to allow the man in maroon scrubs to enter and busy himself with unlocking Mary's gurney for the ride.

"Don't worry, I'm fine," Mary reassured Alex. "This isn't anyone's fault. Shit happens, right?"

"Right." Alex smiled weakly. "Take care. Feel better."

"Thanks for stopping by." Mary waved as the transport tech wheeled her out into the hall and toward the elevators.

Alex stepped out of the room, where Richard Linc was waiting for her.

"Rich." Alex acknowledged the on-call anesthesiologist with an air of caution, fully anticipating a stern reprimand for her actions earlier in the shift with Dr. Jamison in the OR.

Instead, the usually stoic and somber Linc uncrossed his arms and extended a long gangly hand toward Alex, pulled her close and turned her to walk with him as he guided her gently by the shoulder. The gesture was fraternal and in no way threatened Alex as an invasion of personal space, nor could it be construed as sexual.

Twelve years her elder at forty-four, the happily married nerd of a man was consummately professional in all of his interactions and what he may have lacked in personal appearance and demeanor, he more than made up for in clinical brilliance and social grace.

"How you doin'?" he asked, inflecting his over-the-top impression of the stereotypical Southside Chicago drawl. The question, sincere; the characterization, meant to elicit a smile. Both had succeeded.

Alex shrugged against his draped arm and sighed, "Okay."

They passed through the automatic doors at the ER's threshold and crossed the nearly empty lobby in silence. At the elevator, Richard pressed the "up" button and waited. He hugged her close once, firmly.

God bless, you Dr. Linc.

Of his many qualities, Richard knew when not to talk about things. Of her many colleagues, she would miss him the most.

"So, you want to order a pizza from Ant-any's?" Again, the drawn-out syllables of the name "Anthony" brought a smile to her face. The elevator doors opened with a soft chime. They stepped into the empty conveyance.

"Extra 'sass-age'?" she asked, offering her own imitation of the colorful Southside dialect that they both found warmly amusing. The doors whispered closed as they shared a healthy laugh, filling the elevator car with a brief breath of life and a glimmer of lightness.

Four

"That's OB," Linc announced as he glanced down at his pager. He folded the last slice of pizza into his mouth and brushed the crumbs from his hands onto the empty cardboard. As he rose, a few more crumbs fell from the creased lap of his soft blue scrubs and onto the worn carpet of the call room floor. He spoke to Alex around a mouthful of cheese and dough.

"I'll take that, if you wouldn't mind heading down to ER and checking in with Newsome. There's another 'Doe' in trauma holding. This one's a John."

Alex balled up her napkin, threw it into the short waste can and reached for her can of pop.

"Sure," she answered tiredly. "What is it?"

He turned as he slid the door open, "Stab wound. Belly."

She nodded and began folding the empty box.

Dr. Linc left, the door whispered closed, and Alex was left alone with her immediate thoughts.

The image of the woman—Kathleen—twelve hours post-op, wild-eyed and pale, swatting at the side of Mary's head dominated Alex's mind. She recalled the frightfully calm, emotionless voice filling the tense air of the ICU as Kathleen spoke in cryptic phrases.

She remembered the woman's eyes as moist swollen balls of white flesh, unblinking and full of desperation. There had been real malice in the depths of those abysmal pupils, aged and wise. But there was also a flash of innocent curiosity not unlike that of a child.

A child. The bitch killed her own children.

Alex shivered at the thought of Kathleen's thin, knobby-knuckled fingers wrapped around the young tender throats of her victims. She wondered if, at that critical moment, when balanced at the fringe of Death's threshold, Kathleen had stared into their struggling, suffocating faces with those enigmatic eyes? Was that erie glint of curiosity the driving force behind her deeds, or was there something more sinister at work behind those dilated portals?

And what had gone through those young, innocent minds as mommy squeezed the life out each?

Oh, Christ.

One thought obviously—unavoidably—begat another and soon Alex was swallowing hard against the rising memory of her own vanished daughter. Her thoughts turned reluctantly toward the memory of the missing girl. The deep pain of her loss paled in comparison only to the guilt that welled up and washed the sorrow away.

Cora's disappearance was, indirectly or not and as a simple matter of fact, entirely Alex's fault.

The memory of that Memorial Day weekend was a clear, bitter etching in the frosted crystal of her soul.

~ * ~

The cool Friday afternoon had slid smoothly into an unseasonably hot weekend that particular May; and by noon on Sunday, the intensity of the white sun had bleached the clear dome of blue sky. A thin haze had hung in the air and the breeze remained negligible. A perfect day for the beach.

After packing their extra large towels, sun-screen, beach-wraps, and flip flops; Alex had turned to the cooler: Two bottled waters, a few juice boxes for Cora, some grapes and Bing cherries in plastic Ziplocs, and the extra-large one-and-a-half liter sports bottle filled with strong rum-and-Coke. Enough ice to cover the load, and an extra flask of the remaining Bacardi finished off the medium-sized green and white Coleman.

Alex had never given the alcohol a second thought, it was simply part of the packing list for a day at the beach; an afternoon of relaxing in the sun after a long week, sipping a cold drink and watching Cora frolic in the waves.

And so they left for the shores of Lake Michigan, traveling just north of the city to a smaller park Alex knew of, away from the throngs of younger flesh that would crowd onto the limited sand at the Oak Street and North Avenue Beaches

The beach at Illinois State Park was a narrow strip of rocky sand north of Waukegan, between Zion and the Wisconsin border. The area was less popular than the more trendy Chicago beaches, and as a result usually less crowded.

Cora had sat quietly in the backseat, reading her books and sipping on a strawberry shake from Burger King. From time to time, Alex would gaze admiringly at her in the rearview, between sips from her own cup of diet Coke spiked with a generous splash of rum.

Again, at that time, Alex thought nothing of the act of drinking while driving. After all, she was only sipping, slowly melting away the week's stress, smiling at her lovely five-year-old and smoothing herself into a soft mellow buzz. Just enough—she told herself confidently during the forty-minute ride—to maintain plasma-concentration and an overall healthy glow. She was a professional, after all, well versed in the fine art of titrating-to-effect.

Together mother and daughter had staked out a nice slice of beach real estate equal distance from both the mildly breaking surf and the snack-shack, with just enough empty sand between them and the next plot of colorful blankets to provide a comfortable zone of personal space.

Little Cora spread her large rectangular Dora the Explorer towel with one hand as she absently handed her empty shake cup to Alex with the other.

"Done," she exclaimed.

Alex accepted the empty cup as she suctioned the last of her rum and diet Coke from the bottom of her own ice-filled cup. As she turned to walk toward a wire trash barrel at the edge of the smooth sand, she watched Cora bounce on her towel, alternating legs as she attempted to kick the pink plastic Crocs from her chubby feet.

"Wait for Mommy, Princess Pea," Alex cautioned, anticipating the little one's anxiousness to get wet. Cora was a water bug, naturally at ease in the water since birth.

The small girl sighed dramatically, rolled her eyes, firmed her brow and fisted her little hands on her hips.

"I'm not a Princess today!" she admonished. "Today, I'm Cora the Explorer. And we hafta get Boots and go into the ocean to find Map." The little girl gestured toward the inland sea that was Lake Michigan, her gaze intent and impatient.

"Okay, okay," Alex answered as she pitched the soggy cups into the trash. "Let me get ready."

Once back on Cora's beach towel, Alex toed off her own flip-flops, squatted out of her thin nylon shorts and ran her fingers quickly along the hem of her swim briefs, pulling them out of her ass-crack. She ignored the collection of obvious stares and furtive glances from the surrounding male sunbathers, yet took silent pride in her ability to still turn heads. Her bikini was Victoria's Secret, her trim body a result of daily afternoons at Bally's and her confidence was fueled by Bacardi. The mild buzz allowed her enough loose social latitude to smile openly at her own healthy dose of narcissism. She pulled her straight shoulder-length hair into a quick ponytail and then took Cora's eager hand.

Together, they bounded down the sand to the water, trotting across the hot silica in hops and skips. Cora screeched with unrestrained delight; Alex's smile widened as her daughter's face flushed with raw joy.

They played in the bubbly surf, splashing and clinging to one another. They stood in the cool, soft slurry of sand at the interface of water and beach, allowing the easy surges to wash over their feet and slowly bury their toes with each passing swell.

The flare of the sun lit the tiny crests of the fresh-water waves like flint-split jewels, glinting and flickering in the hazy afternoon air. In the reflected sun flashes, Cora's short blond banana curls would periodically blaze with white fire, framing her round porcelain face in a golden halo. Her deep ice-blue eyes cemented the angelic image, and for the moment, Alex was certain that even Heaven itself could not be completely responsible for such a sight.

It grew hot, and soon Cora became thirsty. So had Alex.

They emerged from the water as graceful as mermaids, tiptoeing as if on newly acquired feet, mother carrying daughter when the sand became too dry and searing for the little one's tender feet.

Back at their site, Cora sprawled on her towel sipping from a juice box as Alex spread a generous amount of clear sunscreen on the little girl's arms, legs, shoulders, and back.

When complete, she wiped her hands on the towel, opened her beach chair, turned it to face into the brilliant sun and reached earnestly for the cooler.

Recumbent in her chair, the tall sport bottle of spiked cola sweating in her lap, Alex laid her head back and closed her eyes behind her wide sunglasses as she listened to her daughter softly narrate her own made-up story to the pictures in a book she brought. Her sweet, innocent voice lulled Alex into a daydream as she rhythmically tugged at the plastic sipping straw with her thin, moist lips. The icy drink both cooled and warmed with each swallow, and soon that familiar and comfortable blanket of numbness enveloped her limbs and nestled at the back of her mind.

She only realized she had dozed off when Cora woke her with a less-than-gentle tweak of her right nipple and an insistent prying open of her eyelids. Alex twitched with a start, and shook her head.

"Mommy!" her five-year-old chided. "Wake up, Mommy! I'm hungry."

Alex stretched, glanced at her watch and weighed the sport bottle in her grasp. It sloshed heavily, more than half full, the ice not even melted. She had only drifted for a few minutes, but it felt as if she were waking from a powerful nap. She yawned and answered Cora.

"Alright, baby. Hot dog or cheeseburger?" she asked, not actually knowing what choices the snack-shack had to offer, but rather assuming that the usual beach fare would prevail.

Cora wrinkled her nose and shook her head, round cheeks puffed into her trademark Princess-pout. Alex sighed, stretched again and placed the drink bottle in the sand as she reached for her small beach bag and the wallet within.

"All right then, let's go check it out".

Hand in hand, they hopped and skipped across the scorched sand toward the faded brown concession stand.

The cracked and split wood of the small shed-like structure had been baked dry. The single, wood-framed door hung askew on rusted hinges, the mesh of the torn screen flapped lazily in the mild lake-front breeze. Alex pulled the door open and guided Cora across the threshold. The air inside was stale, redolent with the sweet aroma of marijuana.

A longhaired man in a blue bandana and knee-length surf shorts sat on the chipped, white reach-in freezer against the far wall. His white t-shirt was dingy—stained at the armpits and ripped along the seams. He was tall and thin, yet his arms tensed with corded muscle as his fingers worked at braiding the frayed end of a manila-hemp rope. Though he was partly in shadow, Alex sensed his sleepy gaze drift to the smooth crease of her cleavage as she stepped onto the uneven decking that served as the snack-shack's floor. She assisted Cora up the small step and led her into the hot shadows.

The man dropped from his perch and ambled out from the darkened rear of the shop. He rested his bony hands on the flecked white linoleum of the counter as he leaned forward, gently twirling the loose braids of rope with his fingers. His single blood-shot eye bounced slightly, dysrhythmic with the telltale nystagmus of acute intoxication, wavering between Alex's breasts and the beaming smile of the vibrant little girl at her side.

His other eye was concealed behind a homemade patch of faded black felt and a thin cord of white cotton. He had drawn crude targeting cross-hairs—like those within the scope of a rifle—on the patch in Day-Glo orange. A jagged scar ran from beneath the corner of the eye patch, across his cheek, down the side of his neck, and extended under the stretched-out collar of his tee shirt. It made his face seem rugged—mysterious. Even sexy, in a dangerous, forbidden way.

Somewhere behind the counter an oscillating fan hummed, blowing soft waves of cool air across the interior of the store. Cora's hair feathered in the fan's breeze.

Alex allowed a soft, easy smile to awaken her face as the rum-fueled ball of warmth in the center of her brain swelled and reminded her of her own thick buzz. That and the mild euphoria of another's appreciative glance—even if he was older and bit creepy—lifted her self-awareness to lofty heights. Her nipples hardened in the fan's gentle turbulence. Without hesitation, her self-control inhibited by the rum and teased by instant dreamy fantasies, she felt herself hopelessly, almost hypnotically flirting with the man. That disembodied, airy numbness lasted for only a second or two before Cora's voice hooked and reeled her back.

"What does it say, Mom?" Cora pointed to the dry-erase board propped against the cooler. The snack-shack's Spartan menu was hand printed in blue and green smears, the letters randomly alternated from lower-case to caps and then back.

At the word "Mom", the man cocked his head, stood upright and crossed his thin arms in front his lean chest. His one eye twitched and then refocused, sharper than previously, as he took a few full seconds to size up Alex. His appraisal was deep, almost fastidious, and when he blinked and returned to meet her gaze, his easy smile pled seduction.

His teeth were crooked and irregular, but clean and an even shade of ivory. They seemed too large for his narrow mouth. A reptilian quick dart of his tongue dragged a thin blot of frothy saliva to the cracked corner of his mouth.

The instant suffocation of impending threat grew as a heavy swell in Alex's belly and her inebriated mind conjured all of the possible thoughts that could be racing through the man's head:

Not bad, for a MILF topped the imagined list.

She suddenly realized her mistake, instantly ashamed of her carelessness. A wave of paranoia washed through her as she looked away from the man. Her protective instincts were muddied by alcohol and her mind staggered to re-establish nominal perception.

"Mom," Cora pleaded, verging on the edge of a whine. "What does it say?"

"Just a sec, Cora!" Alex snapped and was instantly ashamed. Her daughter flinched and then stared open-eyed at her mother. Alex took a deep breath. The euphoric wave of her buzz had swollen into impatient agitation and bitter resentment; the former with herself for allowing the booze to loosen her vigilance, and the later at the ever predictable male response to her and her place in the world.

Her thoughts were fuzzy, racing and disjointed. She suddenly wanted nothing more to do with this creepy dude running the snack shop, the gawking sunbathers, Dr. David Rose, or any other fucking Man.

Shit! she screamed silently. The moment eased by and she eventually regained some degree of control.

I'm a little fucked up, here.

She tried to focus her brain away from drunk and on toward calm. *Better slow down on the Rum-and-Cokes. Get a bite to eat.*

She smiled weakly at the man behind the counter, yet held herself somewhat poised and unsteadily concentrated on maintaining a stoic, confident facade. She tried to ignore his cycloptic and lecherous glimpses at her bosom, the ragged scars on his face, the eye-patch; and squinted to read the smudged lettering of the menu. The ink seemed more blurred to her now than previous.

"We'll have two cheeseburgers, chips, and water." She noticed that the words had slurred only after they fell out of her mouth, the c's and s's sliding across her drunk tongue. The man nodded, seeming not to notice any impediment. He was eyeballing Cora now.

"Mom," Cora whispered as she tugged gently on Alex's hand. Alex looked down at her daughter, blinking quickly to bring the little blonde into focus.

"Hmm?" she cooed, trying for a gentleness to smooth over her abrupt retort earlier.

"No mustard, remember? Or pickles. Just 'chup."

"Yes, hon." Alex smoothed the tiny girl's frizzy hair with her hand. The feel was like warm corn silk.

"Ketchup only for one. The works for other." She directed the man, whom had already sauntered over to the glass-encased warmer to fish out the pre-wrapped sandwiches.

He returned, handed her the paper-swaddled burgers and two small bags of chips then pointed over Alex's left shoulder. His eye tracked slowly, his face now slack and bored, no longer interested in Alex or her boobs.

"Condiments are over there, water's in the cooler by the door. Help yourself." He nodded as if to first reinforce this information and then to agree with himself.

"Six dollars, even," he said. His voice was deep and attractive; a stark contrast to his damaged face.

Alex snared a five and a one out of her thin wallet and fed them over; the bills flipped gently in the breeze of the blowing fan. She continued to avoid eye contact, yet the man seemed not to care. He was preoccupied with watching Cora as she bounced from one foot to the other, mouthing the words to some song while twirling her golden hair.

Alex waved the money in front of the man's face. He blinked his solitary eye twice, pursed his lips and then carefully slid the bills from her loose fingers without shifting his gaze. When his fingers brushed against hers, Alex shivered as if a thousand geese had run over her grave. She quickly reached for Cora and turned to leave. The heat of the man's monocular stare bore into their backs. She pulled Cora in front of her in a weird attempt to shield her daughter from the poison of his glare with her own body.

As they walked away, the man sneezed once. Alex, out of polite habit, glanced over her shoulder to offer a quiet "geshundheit" but the blessing froze in her throat at the sight of his other eye. He had lifted the patch and was gently massaging the reddened flesh around the hazy dead oculus. He smiled crookedly and nodded a menacing farewell.

She led Cora back to the entrance where she quickly dressed their cheeseburgers, secured their bottled waters and then held the door for her daughter as they stepped out into the blinding whiteness of the day.

"Can I have an ice-cream?" Cora asked they passed a cartoon advertisement for Dove bars taped to the outside of the snack stand. Alex glanced at the sun-bleached poster of a polar bear dressed in a ski hat and mittens, offering a Dove bar on a stick. She stole a quick glimpse back at the man in the store, leaning against the squat freezer, arms folded across his narrow chest, smiling at them from beneath his twisted eyepatch.

"Can I?" Cora repeated.

Alex sighed, shaking her head in both disappointment and disgust at her internal behavior. She knew she had issues. Man issues. But why she always reacted so impulsively, so viscerally, still remained a mystery to her. Yet this creepy fuck in the snack shop left her with a sobering sense of dread.

"Please," the little girl begged.

"You finish all of your burger, then we'll see. The whole thing, this time, 'kay?"

Cora jumped up and down three times, smiling with the certainty that only children have, imagining an inevitable ice cream in her future regardless of the amount of stale cheeseburger left remaining in the steam soddened wrapper twenty minutes from now. She reached for her mother's hand as she danced in place.

They walked back toward their towels and chair, Alex carried their lunch in both hands as Cora gripped her wrist and led her across the blazing pale sand.

Cora tore into her burger, ravenous and quiet. Alex added ice to her bottle of Bacardi and Coke, her own burger forgotten on the sand beneath her chair. She sipped and grimaced at the dusty taste of the stale, watered-down drink. She re-opened the cooler, scooped the half-emptied flask of rum out from the ice-bath and spun the cap off, letting it fall into the water with a dull plop.

Without a conscious thought, the decision made deep within her psyche, she emptied the contents of the flask into her sport bottle. The liquid within was now a sick, pale caramel color, with only enough cola to give the concoction the faint hue. She dropped the empty glass bottle into the cooler with a splash, snapped the lid closed and leaned back into her reclined chair. She swirled the contents of her plastic bottle to mix them, then took a long draw from the thick plastic straw. She grimaced again, this time a slight shiver ran down her neck while her cheeks cramped slightly from the potency of the iced rum. When the sting of the liquor faded and her mouth warmed, she clenched her teeth against the satisfying numbness of her gums. She calmly calculated she would have to consume about half of the sport bottle during the next few minutes to return herself to the comfortably numb state she had lost during the past thirty minutes. She took another long sip, tolerating the sting much better now.

She absently toed her flip-flops with her right foot as she burrowed her left into the sand. Pleasantly surprised at how the sand was remarkably cooler a mere three inches beneath the surface, she toyed with the distant memories of some random scientific equations to account for the thermal variances.

She smiled to herself as she sipped, the weird social interplay between the concessions man nearly forgotten. She casually justified the surge of irresponsible alacrity followed by her subsequent crash to earth as a mere brush with the usual minor league demons patrolling the fringes of drunkenness. Even the menace of the one-eyed freak became diluted in her mind as she swam back into the waters of inebriation.

She listened to Cora hum as she played in the sand; the tune was familiar yet the name eluded Alex. She shifted in her chair, took a long pull from the straw, closed her eyes and savored the burn of the spicy rum. She began to hum along with Cora, hoping that the name of the tune would coalesce from memory.

A cloud drifted in front of the sun, eclipsing the beach, dragging a cool gray shadow across Alex's upturned face.

The Grand Old Duke of York! That was it.

But was that the actual title? Her thoughts were thick and gauzy now, yet her internal voice remained articulate and sharp.

He had ten thousand men. He marched them up and down the hill, and then marched them back again.

As Cora continued to hum, Alex murmured the next lines aloud, thickly slurring the words as she drifted into a deep warm cocoon of intoxication.

"'And when you're up, you're up. And when you're down, you're down. And when you're only halfway up, you're neither up nor down'".

Alexandra D'Meiter passed out with less than a third of her iced drink warming in her sport bottle. The green container rested on her flat stomach balanced loosely between her interlaced fingers, the condensation trickled down the sides of the plastic and pooled in the tiny concavity of her pierced navel.

~ * ~

The black flies arrived late in the afternoon, with the heavy cloud cover and a push of humidity that paved the way for an approaching storm. Bite after bite was incorporated into her dream until the waking nip stung the tender skin of her inner thigh. Alex slapped her leg, and then brushed it softly, feeling the raised welt.

She opened her eyes and squinted against the gray light filtering through the growing overhead gloom. Her sunglasses hung askew from her left earlobe, rocking as she stiffly pushed herself upright in the chair. The intense radiance of the sun was gone and the air was tacky and stale with growing humidity, the atmosphere charged from a distant storm that rolled across the metallic waters of the great lake.

Another fly bit the top of her small toe and she slapped at it, annoyed and slightly disorientated. Her sunglasses fell to the sand with a dull click as the bows closed upon themselves.

"Fuck," she croaked. The remnants of her dream abruptly faded from lucidity like fog burning off in the maturing dawn. The fly bites rekindled a feeling of being poked and prodded in her dream, something akin to needle jabs, like shots or IVs.

Alex rubbed her face and blinked a few times, instantly regretting her failure to properly sunscreen herself. Her eyelids felt like dried leaves and stung with each effort as they creased, folded and unfolded. The skin beneath her puffy eyes and across her brow burned, pulled as taut as the skin of a marching drummer's snare.

Marching, she thought—remembering. *Marching men. The Grand Old Duke of York had marched ten thousand men.*

Cora. Where is Cora? Oh my God!

In that instant, Alex collectively thought of everything and nothing at once. The crystal clarity of her realization that Cora was missing condensed into a black vacuum, thrumming in the center of her chest.

More *beyond* the center, actually; in a place that until that day she never really believed existed.

Philosophers and theologians have debated for ages about the existence of the human soul—whether or not it had substance, occupied space and physically influenced the corporeal body. Or was it merely a concept—an intangible hypothetical constructed to placate human insecurities? Poets, authors and musicians have all written about events that chill, lift, and crush the soul; as if it did, in fact, exist in some material way.

It was at that very moment, when Alex's sun-tortured eyes looked through the glaze of hung-over eye-snot and saw a crumpled and empty Dora the Explorer beach towel covered in a spray of sand, that she was certain—beyond all doubt—that there was indeed a place within us all where the soul actually resided.

Because when that particular point within her instantly shriveled and knotted into an irretrievable density of absolute ice, she knew on a level that terrified her with cold certainty she would never see her daughter again.

That snapshot of clarity shattered as abruptly as it had formed; the calm and rational framework of absolutes was instantly shrouded by a thick film of panic and terror.

Alex scrambled upright, tangled her feet in her towel and the chair, fell forward, and planted her face in the grainy sand. Her sport bottle tumbled from her lap and landed upside-down in the sand. For a strange, long second she stared stupidly at the green plastic bottle; bubbles chugged within as the remaining rum and Coke leaked past the capped straw and saturated the surrounding sand.

She rolled and hopped gracelessly to her feet, spinning around frantically, spitting sand from her mouth, scanning the now nearly deserted beach. She tried desperately to scream Cora's name, but literally could not find her voice. Tears of fear and frustration erupted in a torrent, her nose ran and thin tendrils of saliva flew from her lips.

"Cora!"

Her raspy voice finally burst forth from lungs too tight to re-inspire and for a single second she felt as if she might actually pass out. Hazy dots danced across her vision; graying out at the periphery as a dull, insistent pressure swelled behind her eyes. She doubled over and forced the blood into her head with a modified Valsalva maneuver, clenching her stomach and bearing down. The vertigo of vagal stimulation passed, and she swam back into consciousness.

"Cora Rose!" she bellowed again, the sound of terror in her own voice caused goose flesh to rise over her entire body.

Alex finally broke into a run. Scanned the beach. The water. The surrounding woods. She yelled. Screamed until her voice cracked. She frantically asked the few remaining beach dwellers if they saw anything, anyone. To a person, they all shook their heads solemnly, and continued to pack their things, secretly thanking God they weren't the ones flailing against all possible hope in search of a missing child.

The concession stand had closed, the beach was quickly emptying, and the storm loomed large on the low horizon. Flashes of lightning ignited the upper blooms of the roiling thunderheads. Alex sprinted barefoot and erratic into the thin spread of trees that surrounded the beach, absently thinking the woods may not be the safest place during a lightning storm.

She spent the next two hours scouring the beach, the surf, and the woods for any sign of Cora. When the rain came, it came hard and persisted throughout her search into the darkening dusk. She screamed herself hoarse and ran herself limp. Cataracts of water poured from the black sky, bent and throbbing from the wind. The lake waters swelled from the gusts. Hot blue lightning arced across the veil of the heavens.

One of the last departing beach dwellers must have taken mercy on Alex and phoned the police. Eventually, steady red and blue strobes counter-reflected the frequent flashes of lightning as a cruiser pulled to the edge of the flooded park. Sand flowed in torturous pseudo-rivers as the deluge carved away at the once smooth beach.

Two troopers emerged from the car, standing in the open doors, clad in heavy rain gear. The whipping skeins of rain pelted the men, the roof of the cruiser, the interior. One of the men attempted to call to Alex over the vehicle's external PA system, but the storm swept away his words.

The passenger eventually stepped clear of the car and slammed his door against the gale. The driver ducked back in behind the wheel and pulled the door closed after him. The police officer bent over at the waist, leaned into the sweeping sheets of rain and shuffled through the sandy quagmire toward the breaking surf, where a dim silhouette stumbled about. She was illuminated by the rhythmic pulses of the police strobes as well as backlit from the periodic burst of low atmospheric discharges; a jerky specter that trance-walked along the foamy silver surf.

Lightning flashed in quick succession as Alex collapsed into the frothy green-black water, pitching forward in a clumsy bundle.

~ * ~

The elevator doors opened with a squeak, and Alex stepped from the conveyance—out of her past—and back into reality; leaving the bitter, horrible memories of that day behind.

For now.

She sighed and walked across the lobby toward the emergency department door. As she approached, the triage nurse noticed her through the thick glass of one of the windows and nodded a greeting. Alex swiped her badge across the small black reader at the threshold and the wide door swung open silently. The triage nurse rounded the corner in a controlled rush and waved Alex over. When the women were standing together, the nurse then motioned to a third person.

A police officer stepped from behind a partially closed curtain and approached the two women, sipping from a small vending machine cup of coffee. The aroma filled the air, and Alex made a mental note to brew up a pot when she returned to the call room.

"This is officer Chandry," the triage nurse announced excitedly. Her voice was a little tense, her face tight, and her eyes narrowed almost conspiratorially.

She lowered her voice to a whisper. "He brought in our homeless John Doe." She paused, arching her brow dramatically. Alex calmly flicked her somber gaze from nurse to cop and back.

"Along with a survivor from the alley apartment," the nurse added before dropping the bomb.

"A baby."

~ * ~

"All we know after that is he somehow made it to the ER on his own and collapsed in the ambulance bay. He must've carried the baby the whole way," Officer Chandry finished explaining to Alex. The three walked slowly toward a drawn curtain across the threshold of the trauma bay.

"He damn near bled out," the nurse added. "That must be, what, ten full blocks?"

The cop nodded as he sipped his coffee. They had reached the boundary of the heavy brown canvas curtain and stopped in a modified huddle outside of the room.

"His blood was all over the scene. Besides, he actually admits to shooting that other woman. They struggled and he was stabbed. He says he rescued the little guy from the dumpster, but knew nothing of the others." He shook his head and sighed, rubbing at his stubbled chin.

"Claims that some calling urged him to the scene. *Pushed* him there. That he was 'needed'." The cop furrowed his brow and pouted his lips in obvious disbelief. "Friggin' crack heads", he mumbled.

The nurse slapped the officer on the arm and abruptly scolded him. "Hey now, watch that tone." Then to Alex she whispered: "I think he might be retarded or something". She arched her eyebrows as she pinched her lips tight.

Alex frowned and looked at the tall police officer.

"No, not him!" The nurse corrected quickly. "Although..."

The police officer suddenly got that he was the butt of the accidental joke and stuck his tongue out at the nurse.

Alex shot him a quick impatient look and then turned to the nurse. "What makes you say that?"

"I don't know, really," the nurse answered. "I mean, it's more in the way he spoke than the way he looks. And his eyes. He just seems... simple." The nurse shrugged.

"What's his status?" Alex asked tersely.

The nurse flinched, caught up in the drama and gossip; she had seemingly forgotten that a trauma patient lay beyond the drape in critical need of their intervention. Her face shifted and she seemed to reboot back into caregiver mode.

"He's getting the second of three units packed-cells; though he's still tachy and hypotensive. With oxygen by facemask his sats are viable. Labs suck, though. Malnourished and anemic, obviously. The guy looks like death warmed-over."

Alex nodded impatiently, asking more specifically, "Can he talk, though? Is he with the program?"

The nurse blinked dully, then responded curtly. "Yeah, sure."

"Thanks." Alex swept the curtain aside and entered the darkened trauma bay, leaving the cop and the nurse outside.

A shadowed form lay still in the bed, illuminated only by the dim neon tracings of the monitor mounted on the wall above the head of the bed. The only sounds in the room were the steady muted hiss from the oxygen mask and the rapid beep of a racing pulse.

Alex approached, eyeing the luminous values of the patient's vitals on the monitor. John Doe remained unmoving under the lightweight sheets. Alex cleared her throat and swallowed thickly against the sudden tightness of fear that clutched her chest. She couldn't rationalize this anxiety, yet the sense of reverse vertigo felt familiar, somehow. Almost like déjà` vu.

"Sir? My name is Alex. I'm from the anesthesia department."

No response. No movement.

"Sir?"

Alex stood to the right of the bed, her hand tentatively resting on the cool metal of the raised side rail. She leaned into the shadows over the bed to try and get a closer look at the man's face. As her eyes adjusted to the low light, his features clarified out of the murk.

Alex caught her breath. An audible gasp escaped her constricted throat like helium rushing from a loosened knot on a balloon.

The man's eyes were wide open, stern and unblinking. They rotated in tandem smoothly to the right and locked onto Alex's own surprised stare. In the moment it took for his pupils to rhythmically contract and dilate with the effort of focusing, Alex recognize the familiar surge of both terror and knowledge in those deep eyes as the same fearful gaze of the woman from upstairs in ICU. Yet, they lacked the menace and insanity.

His eyes were anything but *simple.*

"Now you know, don't you?" the man asked in a raspy whisper. Alex simply stared, unable to answer.

"You've seen her and now you know," he softly answered his own inquiry.

Alex shot a quick, nervous glance toward the closed drape. The cop and ER nurse were gone. There was no one perched outside of the room. She turned back to the unblinking glare of Mr. Doe. She gently slid the face mask up the bridge of his nose, letting it rested on his forehead.

"What do I know? Who are you?" Alex asked quickly, desperately.

The man tried to smile but the effort seemed painful and out of context. He licked his lips. His nose flared with a deep inhalation.

"The baby?" he asked. "Is the baby safe?"

"Yes, he's fine," Alex lied. She never thought to ask how the baby was, but assumed the nurse would've told her otherwise.

"You did great. Brought him in the nick of time." She hoped this would encourage the man to elaborate.

He only smiled again, this time the emotion spread naturally across his pale face. Loosing their distant vacancy for a moment, his eyes filled with moisture and sadness. He blinked slowly and purposefully, dry-swallowed and then reopened his eyes. When he had recaptured Alex's gaze, he spoke clearly and calmly, with the conviction of a sage prophet. His eyes now gleamed with power and emotion she could not easily define.

"You know because you share," he began. "You have also lost, haven't you?" He reached for Alex's hand, took a firm grasp of her first three fingers and squeezed.

"The pain never leaves. I can see it in the lines of your face." He sighed. "Mothers never let go."

Alex's heart froze in mid-stroke before restarting with a silent bang. She wanted to pull away, to shake her head in defiance, cast off this street loon and rub away the hopeful lies.

But she couldn't.

The truth poured from this man's dark eyes like a hemorrhaging dam, flooding the shallow valley of Alex's emaciated soul. The silence between them lasted only the briefest of seconds, yet screamed through Alex's head like a high-pitched Forth of July rocket. Then a word popped into her head that fully described the emotion she felt flowing from his gaze.

Communion.

The frail man held Alex captive in a claustrophobic cocoon of prophetic anticipation for a moment longer before speaking again.

"It doesn't have to end with your Cora Rose." He smiled warmly, yet with a stern countenance and then continued, "In fact, it shouldn't."

Alex stared in disbelief, torn between terrified revulsion and mystical curiosity.

He couldn't possibly know about Cora. What's going on here?

"There is something you can do," the man suggested, his eyes pleading, still moist. "You can still take action."

The man closed his eyes and sighed; his face sunken and drawn with exhaustion. When he reopened them, his eyes were cold and commanding, nearly void of color.

Those eyes terrified Alex; yet she peered into them as if through a rip in time, unable to resist their firm gaze.

"You must find a way into the Crease," the man whispered. "Find *yourself* there, and learn from the Devices."

Eric McBride licked his lips and then continued, "With her gone now, the one-eyed man is next. There is always only one; and he is *yours* as she was *mine*."

Then he passed out. It wasn't until his hand went limp with unconsciousness, that Alex realized she had been squeezing the man's fingers to the blanching point. When she released her grip, his hand slid gently onto the clean white linen.

Alex worked the cramp from her own hand as tremors of emotion worked their way from her empty core. She hesitated and then fell clumsily into a hard plastic chair at the bedside.

A dark, hollow wave washed over her. She cried softly into her hands.

Five

The Crease

Alex packed in two days, layering her life between bubble wrap and newspapers and then stacking the large plastic totes in the rented U-Haul trailer or in the back of her Ford Expedition. The trip to Michigan should normally take only five hours, traveling the direct route through Indiana and then skirting around the eastern edge of Lake Michigan. But she instead decided—quite impulsively, after watching an episode on the Travel Channel—to strike out due north through Wisconsin and into the Upper Peninsula of Michigan. This alternate route would cost her at least twelve hours; but the UP seemed to offer a brand of wilderness and seclusion that quietly called to her. She was enchanted by the images of the great pines and sparkling rivers that snaked through endless rolling hills.

But it had been the subtle suggestion of terrific winters—a world frosted over in one continuous white crust of snow—that truly mesmerized her. It was a nagging sort of attraction. An itch, really.

Perhaps even an addiction.

She had been methodically boxing her clothes from the two dressers she would leave behind as she watched the small plasma TV mounted on her bedroom wall. When the commercial had ended and the travel program had returned, the narrator's voice took on a distant echoing quality. Alex was in mid-fold of her favorite White Sox jersey when she found herself frozen and staring hypnotically into the flat panel of the Sony.

The images were breath-taking as the camera soared over mound after mound of perfect unbroken snow. In the low sun of some winter afternoon the flaky crystals sparkled like diamond chips on smooth cotton. The narrator droned on but Alex ignored his baritone eloquence; instead she perceived the distant roar and sigh of sub-arctic winds as they whistled across the tundra of the high north. Though she knew she had merely imagined the cry of some winter's storm, the surreal echo nevertheless became snagged on her thorny subconscious as the fabric of her remembered dreams unfolded into reality.

Her dreams painted a very different picture from the ones found on the State of Michigan website. The visions had become more intense since her decision to divorce herself from the Windy City and make an attempt at self-discovery in God's Country, but they were nothing like the horrifying nightmares that followed Cora's disappearance. Those particular terror driven illusions were born of guilt and fueled by self-loathing.

No, these recent fantasies had much more substance to them. There was structure and purpose behind these images.

Memory.

The dreams all shared a common theme: a vast frozen wilderness that surrounded her and filled her with agitated emptiness. It was a palpable void, constructed from heavy black light. She could sense a throbbing power far beyond her perception, tensing and growing, bulging at the bonds tethering it behind some barrier. She could not determine if this power—this sentience—was good or evil, and although she often awoke from the dreams terrified, she still felt strangely calmed by their familiarity. And despite the overwhelming power of the unseen entity, she was never actually intimidated by it, but rather awestruck and curious.

Wanting.

Now, watching the montage of Northern Michigan winterscapes on her TV, Alex felt an intense sense of rightness. It was almost like a flood of déjà vu.

But not quite. This was more like...

Synchronicity. As if she had actually dreamed these places into existence.

Or, perhaps *they* dreamed *her* into being...

That seemed more correct, as she thought about it.

Necessary.

Alex knew then that tomorrow when she pulled away from the curb for the last time, she must travel along the route she had planned. It was simply necessary.

She was being called upon and the absolute virtue of the synchronicity clarified her soul.

~ * ~

That night Alex dreamed again. Essentially the same dream. Although this time the great expansive winter void that dominated her dreamscape wrinkled a little at one corner, allowing a bit of that unseen substance to leak in.

Just a little.

A part of her, ancient and lonely, began to sense the necessity of certain things: the unavoidable consequences of decisions and a purpose behind the fabric of pain that seemed ever present in both dreams and in waking life.

Her dreams. Her life.
The dream...

~ * ~

The sleeper awakes...

...to realize that she is cold and alone and still within a dream.

And somewhat drunk. Crapulent, even.

She giggles childishly at that word—*crapulent.* It's a real word, of that she's certain; and that's what's so funny about it.

Crapulent corpuscles coursed through her cranium.

She snickers again as the alliteration runs freely through her uninhibited mind—renegade bits of loosely retained rhetoric left over from sophomore composition that she freely associates in her waning euphoria.

She attempts to sit up, succumbs to light-headed instability and falls back onto the seat, giggling tiredly. Through the smog of reluctant and pie-eyed wakefulness, she vaguely recalls her rash decision to *un-quit* drinking— a semi-lucid and irrational conclusion made earlier in the evening.

Un-quit. The unexpected fluidity of *that* clever little colloquialism causes her to smile shrewdly. Most people would contend that *quitting* something habitual, like smoking or drinking, is extremely difficult especially if that activity is particularly addicting.

They should try un-quitting sometime.

Un-quitting is not the same as resuming, she postulates to herself. In fact, the two are distinctly, philosophically, different. Resumption of some activity is predicated on the requirement of choice. One simply chooses to light up a cigarette or reach for a beer. The act reinforces the behavior and the cycle resurfaces.

Because quitting, as it applies to the cessation of harmful behaviors, is more about evolving new philosophies; so, too, is the process of *un*-quitting. One must re-engineer their ideologies to accommodate the new anti-quit doctrine. Having been sober for some period of time, one must now develop an entirely new value system to justify a full committal to the act of un-quitting if they are to be successful in completely un-quitting.

She grins adroitly at the absurdity of her musings; obviously the rationale of a drunk. *A drunk in a dream.* Either way, she figures, the behavior and the will to exercise it still involve choice.

And she had chosen to quit quitting.

She simply gave up. It was that clear. She had grabbed the bottle of rum, the car keys, a pack of smokes, and left the party in a flurry of sheer satin skirt-tails.

Now, of course, she lays across the front seat of a borrowed car—dazed and tired; but surprisingly without too serious of a hangover and no worse for wear.

A blizzard screams outside and snow ticks against the glass of the windshield and side windows, yet she can't recall it having snowed earlier in the evening.

Her stomach cinches tight and her heart pauses for a second as she slowly comprehends the snowstorm outside, the wail of the wind, and the supreme darkness beyond. But the car still idles quietly—heat pouring from the vents—and soon the rhythmic vibration of the engine begins to soothe her.

She suddenly feels bad for the friend from whom she borrowed the car. She left in such a hurried mess and without telling him...

Where exactly was she?

In the dream, remember...

She stretches up from the front seat, reaching for the crumpled pack of cigarettes on the dash. Her bare feet bump against her discarded shoes—black cocktail pumps—and slosh in a small puddle of dirty water that has pooled in the passenger's side foot well.

Her fingers fumble a crooked white cylinder from the pack as she pushes the stub of the silver lighter into the dash. She vaguely recalls that her friend doesn't smoke, and she's pretty sure that he frowns upon it in his car.

Oh, well. It's only dream smoke.

Touching the glowing orange of the lighter's element to the quavering tip of the cigarette proves to be more difficult a task than she anticipated; and she's only successful after two attempts and closing one eye.

She struggles briefly to sit upright and eventually props herself against the passenger side door, allowing her head to rest against the cold glass. She takes a long drag from the cigarette and then closes her eyes against the acrid bite of the smoke that coils like a lazy ribbon from her opened mouth. The flavor of the initial drag scrubs away the bitter leftover taste of alcohol.

The storm rages beyond the protective glass of the vehicle's windows; curtains of winter whiteness flail the car from all angles as the howling wind threshes endless clouds of fine-grained snow and thin cords of beaded icy. The frigid song of the tempest surges in persistent waves from a whimpering groan to a baleful shriek.

She stares through the shifting curtains of snow, adjusting her focus to avoid the ghostly reflection of her own face in the side window. The darkness beyond the writhing blizzard is abyssal—as black as the depth of her pupils as they look back upon her from the glass.

When she refocuses her vision, she finds herself mesmerized by the hypnotic eddies of snow that dance against the obsidian. She becomes enchanted by the eerie luminescence of that swirling chalky expanse.

As she watches the pearly kaleidoscope twist outside, she feels a sudden and insistent pressure rise within her head as a distinct presence begins to push into her mind. The foreign sentience grows and swells; at first, like the nagging echo of one's own conscience and then more like an intercepted transmission.

She's initially startled and instinctively wants to resist the unyielding violation but soon finds herself helpless to stop the intrusion. The will of the exotic force presses upon her, envelopes and then caresses her.

Unable to consciously resist, she can sense her mind begin to smoothly unfold. She feels the layers of her soul—the fabric of her essence—peel away like the concentric layers of an onion as the unseen interloper infuses itself. The act is neither physically nor emotionally painful, feeling more like a psychic file-share than a true violation. In fact, her own native awareness becomes suffused with a calming warmth as a blanket of ancient knowledge spreads across her consciousness—a strange sense of secret history made more familiar with each unrelenting pulsation.

Voices, images, and entire concepts explode silently in her mind, leaving behind the glowing embers of memories that aren't entirely hers—fading afterimages—like galactic flashes from a single great cosmic camera.

With a sudden clarity and sobriety that stun her, she sits forward and stares into the wintry maelstrom, her eyes desperately searching for the umbra that has suddenly reached from far across time and shared with her the memories of cosmic antiquity. As she squints into the blinding snow squall, the throbbing presence tightens its grasp on her mind one last time before winking out in an instant and leaving her in a psychic vacuum.

The sudden emptiness in her head echoes with memory and prophecy.

She flinches and then screams, startled by the unexpected clamor of the car's alarm as it suddenly comes to life. The shrill warbles, sirens, and discordant beeps oscillate from somewhere beneath the buried hood of the SUV, setting her newly enlightened awareness on edge and thrusting her back to essentiality.

She drops the half-smoked cigarette between her legs, the long ash hisses as it's snuffed by the snowmelt on the floor. She considers the now departed foreign presence and slowly begins to process the bewildering event.

She runs her hands through her hair, swallows the tight knot of fear that has swollen in her throat, and begins searching behind her seat for the bottle of rum she had brought.

It's then that she realizes the dream is more memory than actual dream.

Six

According to the clock up front it was 4:13. The numbers shimmered like ghostly symbols.

Eric McBride yawned; a long, deep sigh that tapered to a shivering hitch; momentarily drawing his body tight. He found himself once again awake and alert—impossibly, it would seem—in the dream world. Out of place and time, but solid in body, form and mind.

Christ. Not the girl and car again.

She shifted slightly at his side; her tiny body folded close. Her warmth seeped through the thin denim of his cargo pants as she hugged his leg. In her sleep, she had pulled her own legs up under her and curled into a soft roll under the scratchy wool blanket and the collection of discarded old clothes. Her slender fingers, once curled loosely against her cheek, now slid gently down the side of her chin dragging with them a few wispy strands of raven hair.

He stared at the small crescents of her French-manicured nails; the tips painted white, he knew, but in the cast of eerie luminescence from the blizzard outside, they reflected almost pale yellow. And moist, like bone or cartilage.

4:14.

The fluorescent numerals from the dashboard-mounted stereo silently ticked over another minute. The intensity of the glowing display faded as it reached into the shadowed confines in the back of the vehicle; and despite numerous attempts to focus his weary eyes on the digital numbers, they remained shrouded in a halo of bluish-green haze.

Outside, a violent and swirling eddy of white crystalline dust danced across the field of vision offered through the slight curve of the windshield. Great breaths of snow gusted against the windows, momentarily sticking to the tempered glass in fluffy irregular blotches, only to be breezed away again by the turbulent night storm.

He glanced down at her half-hidden face, the sharp lines of her cheekbones and jaw now softened by sleep. She exhaled deeply—a dream sigh.

A dream within a dream.

He certainly found her attractive, yet in a sobering way. She had physical beauty not to be denied. Yet, something in her tragedy and desperation unveiled a solemn delicateness he felt compelled to protect rather than corrupt.

He had a vague sense that in another time, another place— perhaps another life—he should have found her appealing in a physical, *grown-up* way. This seemed like innocent or immature—even naïve—thinking; but in this place, things were different. His *mind* was different.

This woman was dressed in an aura of sisterly preciousness—untouchable and sacred—and though he accepted this, he still puzzled over the sudden and unexpected surge of chivalry washing through him.

He turned his gaze out the vehicle's back window. The twisting ropes of gale-driven snow had become considerably thicker, throwing a fuzzy opaque cataract over the world outside, accentuating the already barren flat landscape he remembered from just hours previous. The night flared and shimmered with eerie ivory limelight, as if each delicate flake held within it some mysterious luminescent property.

She had asked him to describe that quality—that seemingly inherent luminary ability of freshly fallen snow—but at the time he was so overwhelmed by the mysticism of the night, words had escaped him. Now, he merely marveled at the phenomenon; watching the thick flakes swirl and dance like bioluminescent algae surfing the tidal currents in a deep gray ocean.

He turned to the front; the windshield all but completely obscured now as snow piled up on the remaining half of the hood buried in the growing drift. He rose up on one arm, felt along his hip for the phone and was suddenly overcome by a violent cramp seizing his right side. His oblique muscle spasmed and twitched and tears streamed from his clenched eyes. He flexed and attempted to straighten his body, to stretch the fatigued muscle. His breath hissed between his teeth as he fought the burn of the cramp.

At his side, she stirred, swallowed and then fell back into rhythmic sleep.

The cramp began to subside and he was able to stretch within the compact quarters offered by the SUV's rear compartment. He eventually discovered the phone during the repositioning maneuver—unclipped and wedged under his left buttock. He flipped open the thin black cover and glanced at the phosphorescent screen: A no-service icon flashed and two of four bars were lit on the power indicator.

The time was... well, it wasn't displayed.

He frowned and scrolled through various menus to try and call up the time of day. His efforts resulted in nothing but the same wallpaper image of two penguins playing hockey, and the *No Service, Low Power* icons.

His cramp now gone, he pulled himself to a seated position, bowed his head against the low ceiling and pondered her cell phone. His attempts to open the calendar feature of the device were also unsuccessful, as was his effort to activate the GPS beacon.

The clock in the dash of the car wavered in his vision as he refocused on the glowing numerals.

4:20.

He blinked to clear the film of exhaustion from his eyes. Though the malfunctioning phone was strange, more curious still was the fact that he distinctly remembered glancing at the time on the digital stereo right after they had climbed in back with the blanket and the bottle of rum.

It had been the girl's idea to get some rest and conserve heat, so it had made sense to curl up together in the back of the Ford Expedition and share body heat under the worn Mexican-patterned beach blanket. It had never been sexual, and he was again surprised at himself for his unexpected and easy platonic behavior.

Clad only in a thigh length silky skirt and sheer blouse she had snuggled beneath the wool blanket and fallen instantly asleep, her head cradled against his hip. He remembered glancing at the clock over the seat back as his mind bounced through the inexplicable events of the evening.

Earlier, the clock had beamed at him from the front of the already cooling car: *5:15*

He remembered thinking, *AM or PM*? And then his mind raced back to the uncertainty of his even being here.

Wherever *here* was.

He seemed out of place *and* time, and if not for the solidity of the woman next to him, drawing deep sighs in her sleep, he couldn't be certain that he wasn't fast asleep himself; entertaining the convoluted dreams of one whom had fallen through a looking glass or down a rabbit hole.

A quick puzzling thought blazed to light, ignited from the embers of his drowsy mind as he contemplated the logic of the moment and the shimmering numerals of the clock:

4:20.

It had to be either just past four in the morning, or four in the afternoon. And if the blue-green digital numbers of the in-dash Sony told the truth, then according to the Expedition's clock at least eleven hours had passed since he had crawled into the back of the truck with this beautiful stranger.

Eleven hours? Maybe even twenty-three? Or more.

It seemed impossible that such a slice of time had escaped him, particularly because he was quite certain that he hadn't fallen asleep. And he seemed to recall that he had a remarkable sense of time.

He again glanced at the clock.

4:20

Still?

At the very least a few minutes should have transpired while he wrestled with the inconsistencies of the frosty universe surrounding the stranded Expedition.

Yet, the time remained: *4:20.*

The sea green numerals shimmered and danced, their otherwise sharp margins softened by the distance between the dashboard and the very back of the car. Each digit fuzzed as if by a halo of microscopic St. Elmo's Fire.

Time—as depicted by this clock, at least—seemed frozen in a fluorescent foam of photons; an unyielding, fateful constant in an otherwise perpetual night.

In that ghostly green glow her face had appeared porcelain smooth and mysteriously familiar in profile, like a vaguely remembered sculpture in a dimly lit display case. The arcs of her brows crowned wide oval eyes that were dark and sad. Beneath high angular cheeks, her firm jaw supported a thin shelf of narrow, slightly upturned lips she held in an almost perpetual pout.

Her overall presence had seemed both solid and ethereal, a dichotomous meshing of fear and courage infused with melancholy and strength. Her gaze had captivated as much as frightened him; the depth of her eyes pulsed with knowledge and promise. She was radiant with energies that, for some inexplicable reason, made him think about the chasms between mythologies and natural laws.

The atmosphere of overwhelming mysticism and her idyllic visage had combined with the epic slurry of winter's wrath raging outside to engulf him in a tattered blanket of disorientation. He felt abandoned by reality, misplaced on the lower shelf of humanity.

No, more like *displaced*. The difference being as subtle as losing one's eyeglasses entirely versus viewing the world through said glasses, only with the lenses reversed. Suddenly that displaced feeling seemed more appropriate than ever, and for the first time since he could remember, a wave of familiarity crashed through him.

He hadn't always been this perceptive. In fact, he was strangely—disturbingly—certain that before tonight, at sometime, in some place, he was far less cogent than he now seemed to be.

Somehow, he instinctively knew his thoughts were never this clearly organized, his logic never so sound, and his mind never so quiet. That was what struck him most severely—the new serenity within his head. He seemed to remember, vaguely, that his mind had always been filled with distracting urgency.

As his breath plumed around his head, he realized that the temperature inside the car had dropped, but not so drastically that it had become uncomfortable. Cool to cold, but not frigid. Not at all what he would expect if eleven hours indeed had passed without benefit of the car's heater running.

The car had apparently stalled, yet it was only at this moment that he noticed the absence of the reassuring vibration of the idling engine through the floorboard. He thought about crawling to the front and re-starting it, but decided against that for now as his movement and the sound of the engine would be sure to wake her. Instead he rested against the side window, the freezing glass cooling his back through his sweatshirt, and again pondered the mysteries surrounding this evening.

He recalled the elation he had felt as the image of the vehicle slowly materialized from indistinct shadows as he plodded through the white-out, the edges of the SUV becoming more defined and real as he approached by foot.

However, he failed to recall with any degree of certainty or clarity, the details of his walk through the blizzard to that point; yet it was obvious from the desolate expanse surrounding him he must have walked for hours.

From where, he knew not.

This not-knowing should've bothered him, this strange selective amnesia, but the concern evaporated; the thought more like a film of alcohol drying in a breeze than a substantial pool of reason.

He did, however, remember the semi-buried Ford and his first impression of its seraphic occupant.

~ * ~

"Hey, open up!" he had growled past the ragged leather glove stuffed between his teeth. He rapped hard on the driver's side window with the bare knuckles of his right hand while with his left he tried to open the door. It wasn't quite cold enough to freeze the door tight. It was locked.

A piercing siren continued to burp and yelp in rapid, mechanical heartbeats. The shrill chirps, whistles and warbles swam in and out of clarity, fluctuating in the swirling winter gale.

"C'mon, man", he pleaded. "You car alarm's been going off for at least an hour. I heard it a mile back." He glanced back along the path that had brought him here, his once deep footprints now mere shallow depressions as the wake of tidal snow washed over them, like foam on a cold ivory beach.

His glove back on his hand, he again knocked on the fogged glass.

"Look, I can see you in there and it's not getting any warmer out here. How about a few minutes of warmth?" His pleading protests trailed off as he realized just how pointless his argument was. He suddenly felt foolish, yet the act of talking warmed him and kept him from sinking into depression.

"I know you don't want to open up to a stranger—I can appreciate that. But I am not a crazed psycho or murdering vagrant out for a stroll. I'm stranded as well. Like you. Just without the benefit of a vehicle with a frigging heater."

He paused, waiting for a compassionate or sympathetic response from the dark silhouette he was sure he could see cowering within the vehicle. Perhaps it was only a hopeful hallucination. Maybe the cold had already affected him.

Snow-blind, was it? No, that was during the day.

Snow-stupid—now that was a lot closer to the truth.

"Damn," he mumbled.

Clad in dirty, worn-out tennis shoes, he half-kicked, half-missed the door of the Expedition with one numb foot in a dispassionate act of frustration and feeble assertiveness. The glancing blow—a muted thud—dislodged a thin ridge of accumulated snow from along the edge of the Ford's roofline. Irregular tufts of sticky white fell in ribbons to the ground, forming lacy miniature mountain ranges in the smooth powder at his feet.

He thrust his hands deep into the pockets of the outer-layer of pants, hiking up the waistbands of the others as he surveyed the gray and green truck one last time. The vehicle was solidly lodged in a great mound of snow nearly twelve feet high. Though the drifting winter precipitation had made it impossible to discern the boundaries of whatever roadway may have once existed beneath the thick blanket of snow, he could only assume that this particular mound must have been the result of passing plows.

Yet, he had not witnessed any traffic whatsoever over the past few hours, let alone the roaring salvation of a six-wheel-drive diesel powered twin plow.

Sighing, he turned his back on the Expedition and faced into the needles of icy wind and swarms of monster, crystal flakes. He was dressed in layers, yet the cold bit through the ragged coverings.

"That's exactly what he would say, you know." A nervous and shaky voice rode the winds, thin and full of adolescent bravado; a girl's tenor, tight with fear and caution.

He spun back toward the buried vehicle. Heavy exhaust farted from the tailpipe while wispy tendrils of steamy breath curled out of the half opened driver's window.

"If one were a psycho and/or crazed murdering vagrant, that is exactly what he would say," she explained. "That he wasn't." Small fingers gripped the top of the window, over which he caught flashes of wide, bright eyes.

"True," he agreed cautiously, encouraged by her response. "However, in this case I'd have to believe that even the most ardent and dedicated villain would concede to the elements and place the performance of his craft fairly low on his to-do list." He had to raise his voice to a near yell above the whining car alarm. "A distant second to, let's say, active warming and the preservation of limbs from lethal frostbite."

She seemed to consider all points of his argument and he allowed her the time to do so. Just when he was about to launch into a second more desperate plea, the window scrolled up with a weak mechanical whine.

His heart fell, and he became instantly colder. He considered his appearance for the first time: bundled in mismatched tatters and rags, three or four layers of threadbare garments. It was a mystery to him as to why he would've dress in this fashion, but nevertheless, he supposed he couldn't blame her for her cautious reluctance. He looked homeless.

And perhaps he was. He honestly couldn't be certain that he wasn't.

Then the driver's side door swung open, and he could see her sliding over to the passenger side. Small bare feet followed thin bare legs as she pulled her skirt with her.

"I can't get it to shut off," she explained, now her voice loose with emotion. "It's... it's not my car and I have no idea how the alarm works. If you can help shut it off, I'll let you warm up." Her voice quavered and hitched from exhaustion. "If I have to listen to this damn thing one more second, I'll go insane," she confessed.

Waves of heat swam out of the open door, and he could actually feel the warmth stretch its cozy fingers toward him.

He shuffled back to the car, nearly tripping over his own numb feet. His breath plumed in a foggy sigh of gratitude.

~ * ~

Abruptly, the crying alarm snapped off. Without competition, the winter night screamed around them.

He withdrew his hand from beneath the instrument console, just under the ashtray, and laid three small auto-fuses on top of the dash.

"Well, I'm not sure which one it is, but one of these little guys is for the alarm. Some other electrical features of your car as well, I'm afraid".

"It's not my car."

"Yeah, well at least it's still running and the heat's still cranking." He shucked off his gloves and unzipped his sweatshirt, studying her face for the first time since she unlocked the door for him. A weak wave of recognition swept through him—more akin to a tickle—then faded.

He allowed it to pass, unimportantly, as one might ignore a leaf that had blown across a path in a deep wood during the fall. He turned his attention to the dashboard vents, rubbing his chapped hands together in the warm breath that jetted from the black mesh.

A sudden small metallic click caused him to jump and he turned quickly in his seat.

She had a fresh cigarette poised tightly in the corner of her mouth. She reached for the chrome stub of the lighter, unplugged it, touched the glowing orange element to the tip of her cigarette, puffed twice and replaced the cylinder with a smooth click.

"Lighter still works, too," she exclaimed.

She exhaled a deep breath of sweet flavored smoke—the rich, spicy aroma that only comes after the initial lighting of a quality butt.

"Don't suppose you could spare one?" He asked.

"Yeah, sure. Sorry," she blurted nervously. She handed him the pack of lights. He shook out two, returned one and handed the pack back.

She tossed it absently on the dash, knocking the mini-fuses down the defroster vents at the base of the windshield. They rattled a bit then came to rest somewhere in the works beyond the firewall.

"Help yourself," she quietly offered.

He lit his from the dash lighter and sat back, pushing his soaked feet under the floor vent, warming them in the swirling blast of air.

"I really appreciate this," he finally said. "Thank you."

She only smiled, the gesture tired and drawn. Yet her eyes sparkled in the dimness, quick and seemingly between thoughts.

"I'd been walking for quite awhile, I suppose," he explained, attempting to defuse the uncomfortable silence. "Though I can't say for certain how long or from where." His voice trailed off, the foolishness of this statement weighed heavily and he suddenly felt awash with embarrassment. He struggled for words, appropriate phrases or explanations, yet nothing rang true.

He could neither recollect his past extending any farther back from the moment he first saw the snowbound Expedition, nor could he adequately articulate how this fact truly astounded him. He sensed that he should be distraught, frightened and angered by the disorientation; but what he felt instead was a kind of primitive ambivalence. He glanced again at his vagrant attire.

He was lost and shockingly amnesic, yet completely serene.

He caught her calm and quizzical look, met her unblinking eyes for a moment and then felt compelled to offer some sort of homespun rationale. He glanced at his watch, considered the cracked crystal and faded face and sniffed. Pouting and chewing the inside of his cheek, he shrugged.

"Watch must've crapped out in the cold," he mumbled lamely. "From the moisture." He shook his arm and the timepiece rattled and clinked softly.

"I guess I must've run aground somewhere back there and then ran out of gas." He looked sheepishly at her, and then instinctively glanced at the fuel gauge.

Half a tank.

She caught his furtive glance and her smile widened as her features cleared.

"We could make it last a little longer," she said. "Run it long enough to warm the inside, shut it off until we can't stand the cold anymore and then start it up again."

She gently shook her head as she answered her own suggestion. "But I don't dare turn it off now that it's running."

He nodded slowly and stared solemnly past her shoulder at the swirling curtains of snow outside.

"Where were you hoping to get to? Walking, I mean?" she asked.

"I dunno." He sucked lightly on the cigarette. "I guess a house or another car," He turned to her and shrugged.

She arched her brow as if to say *well you found one, now what?*

"What about you?" he finally asked. "Where were you headed?"

She narrowed her eyes and cocked her head, as if contemplating the question, organizing her responses and clarifying what she should or should not share with a total stranger. At first, she appeared angry at the inquiry and he suddenly regretted prying; but then she softened.

A wry smile spread slowly across her face and she chuckled. She leaned toward him into the thin column of smoke that spiraled from the tip of her cigarette. The plume framed her angular face in a wreath of bluish haze.

"I don't know, either," she whispered then shook her head. "I woke up here."

He surveyed her exhausted features—deep and sorrowful—yet soft and somehow very familiar in the green glow of the instrument panel. Another wave of recollection— or recognition—washed over him, vague and tugging. This time it was much more difficult to ignore.

Twisting white sheets of snow thrashed outside.

They sat silent for a while, nursing their cigarettes and staring out of the half-frosted windows.

"How would you describe it?" she asked, breaking the silence.

He casually surveyed the interior of the car, as would most first time passengers in a strange auto, while he considered both her question and the surreal setting. Ragged, chipped sunglasses hung askew from a clip on the driver's side sun visor and a laminated parking permit for some health club dangled from behind the rear-view mirror. The expiration date was May 31st, 2008.

What was today's date?

He looked at the stereo's clock in the middle of the console: 5:04.

A tube of cherry Chap Stick and an abundance of change littered the shallow cup holders between the two front seats. He resisted the urge to pop open the glove box and flip through the contents as he fingered three scratched CD jewel cases wedged along the side of the drivers seat.

"How would you describe it?" she repeated. "The storm, tonight. Any night, really. The snow and that weird sense of brightness and warmth".

He glanced back at her. She was staring out of the passenger window, her forehead nearly touching the frosted glass. He took the opportunity to look her over and noticed for the first time just how long her hair was—just short of reaching her waist as she sat. And dark, almost raven black.

She suddenly turned and met his gaze. He reflexively jerked his admiring eyes away and shrugged like a teen caught in mid-gawk.

"I don't know. How would you?" he countered clumsily.

She shifted in her seat, swinging both of her legs to the left, tucking them under her as she sat side-straddle in the passenger seat. He caught a glimpse of delicate bare feet and a healthy portion of thigh. She made no attempt to adjust the hem of her modest skirt and he was mildly stunned that the situation invoked none of the usual physical arousal he expected. He, instead, felt remarkably ambivalent.

"Reach behind my seat," she directed. "There should be a bottle back there somewhere."

He complied and produced a two-thirds full bottle of Bacardi.

"No Coke", she apologized. "Sorry."

He handed her the bottle. She grasped the neck with one small hand and smoothly unscrewed the cap with the middle finger and thumb of the other. Her fingers were thin and long, tipped with moderate length French-manicured nails.

She visually considered the opening of the bottle for a hesitant moment, staring reluctantly into the smooth glass and then with a defeated sigh, she tilted the bottle to her lips and took a clean mouthful. She made no grimace, only a tiny quake of her shoulders as she swallowed.

She handed the bottle back with a tired adolescent frown, her eyes suddenly vacant and still, stained with shadowy regret.

"Here's to choices," she whispered. Shame and remorse wrestled with her features.

He accepted the bottle and held it with both hands in his lap. He watched her face gently twist and tense as she obviously worked through some difficult thoughts.

"Do you remember your dreams?" she finally asked.

Turning her attention from the window back to him, her eyes were again sharp—nearly piercing—and demanded a captive audience.

He fought to tear his own eyes from her arresting gaze as he brought the bottle to his lips and pulled a cautious first swallow from the fifth. The sharp molasses tang bit his tongue and instantly anesthetized his gums. His eyes watered and he fought the urge to cough as the liquid warmth threw his throat into miniature spasms.

She never blinked, but held his eyes with dramatic intensity as she calmly awaited his response. He sensed her need for an answer and after a moment's recollection he actually remembered the question.

"Yeah, I suppose," he said. "Some."

"They say that you dream more than once whenever you do," she replied. "I don't recall the exact number, but it's a lot." She reached for the bottle and he complied.

"However, you really only remember the last one. Sometimes the first, if it's potent enough; but usually only the last one remains lucid."

She tipped the bottle, more confidently this time and without the remorseful hesitation. She took two long pulls, sucking audibly. The hollow of her neck pulsed with each swallow. When she lowered the bottle, her lips glistened with moisture and her eyes sparkled with surprising clarity.

"They also say that dreams only last a few seconds, even though they can seem to last much longer. Dream-time is relative, I suppose." Her voice seemed polished from the alcohol; not at all tight or breathy, but rather musical.

Not knowing how or when to respond at this point, he simply nodded and let his gaze travel about the car wandering from the tube of Chap Stick to the glowing numerals of the clock and then back. He caught another glimpse of pale flesh as she cradled the bottle between her thighs and was again surprised by the apathy he felt upon glimpsing her exposed legs. As he dropped his gaze down the length of her slender calves he felt none of the stirrings of desire he assumed he should feel—would've felt—had he not found himself in this inexplicable dream-like scenario.

Do you remember your dreams?

Come to think of it, he supposed so. And this was certainly one for the books.

He watched her untuck and then cross her delicate feet as she placed them back on the floor of the passenger side. They came to rest next to a sleek looking pair of black leather pumps laying on their side in a puddle of snow melt slush that had pooled on the rubber floor mat. The tiny crescents of her painted toenails shimmered from the moisture of the puddle.

He glanced up to see her lighting another cigarette. She appeared oblivious to the wetness in which her bare feet now lay. She took a deep drag and then passed the smoke. He accepted.

Her hand dropped back into her lap, caressing the curves of the bottle as she brushed a long wave of dark hair from her face with the other. She suddenly leaned closer to him, tipping the bottle between her knees as she did. She reached for the cigarette.

"I dreamed this, you know," she said dryly as she indicated their surroundings with a roll of her eyes and brow. "You, me, the blizzard. All of it." She fell back into her seat and coughed to clear her throat. The smoke from the cigarette she held pinched between her fingers vibrated as it feathered from the trembling tip.

He waited while she mustered the courage to continue. The air in the car was swollen with cigarette smoke and thick in anticipation of what he sensed could only be a revelation.

Then, as she began to speak, an incredible thing happened. Her exact words suddenly formed in his head like a long forgotten lyrical script suddenly remembered. He heard her twice at once, her actual spoken words dovetailed into his impossible *memory* of the same spoken words.

The real text of her speech coalesced from a thin fog of memories—a phantom litany materializing in exact verbatim in his mind. The internal replay unfolded simultaneously with her speech; the raw data in his head overlapped with her melodious voice in psychic harmony.

The synchronicity was surreal and frightening.

"I remember them all," she told him, staring out of the driver's window behind him, seeming to focus on the past.

"The dreams I have, I remember them all." She turned from the window and again held his eyes captive. Her words echoed in his head as she spoke them aloud.

"Brilliant, vivid revelations..." She sniffed, and then continued, "You ever heard of lucid dreaming?"

He swallowed, wanting to speak, but instead remained silent as to not interrupt the fragile moment, curious to see if the bizarre psychic harmony would continue.

"Forward memories?" She eyed him through the gray haze of smoke.

He sat motionless.

She offered the cigarette and he declined with a weak shake of his head. She shrugged, took one last drag and tossed the butt to floor. It hissed briefly as it drowned in the snowmelt.

"You warming up?" she asked, her voice both soft in his ears and reverberant in his mind.

"Yeah," he answered, slightly bewildered. He was just thinking about feeling warmer. In fact, the outpour of warm air was beginning to sting his toes, though his shoes remained soaked. He tolerated the excessive heat in hope to dry out his sneakers.

She smiled and nodded, as if she already knew his answer, his thoughts.

"Some repeat, but not many," she continued. "They link together, mostly. Like chapters on a DVD. Without sound, though." She furrowed her brow at this and then whispered, nearly mumbling to herself, "Strange, but I never realized it until now... they're all silent. I guess that's how I can tell the difference; that this is not a dream."

The weird synchronicity was fading now, her audible voice and that in his head were diverging, the connectivity slipping.

He finally spoke.

"What do you dream about?" he asked in a weak voice.

She recaptured his gaze and smiled sadly, "Mostly people I've never known in places I've never been." She sighed.

"That's not uncommon," he insisted. "Like déjà vu."

"No, this is very different." She shook her head in mild frustration. "These aren't thin and spacey or vaguely familiar, but more like explosions of reality. These are solid memories of things that have yet to happen. Forward memory."

He chewed the inside of his cheek as he contemplated what she had said. She narrowed her gaze as she watched him consider her statement. Fear and defensive anger colored her face. He recognized her anxiety and raised a hand as he tried to soothe her.

"Relax, relax. I'm not dismissing you. Not after all that has happened tonight." He shifted in his seat and reached for the bottle between her legs, thinking about his own realistic dreams—like this one—and the apparent time and space shift that occurred.

When he brought the bottle forth he couldn't help but notice that it was nearly full. He blinked his eyes and quickly tried to recall just how much rum had been in it to start. He could've sworn it was only two thirds full when he withdrew it from behind the seat. They each had taken swigs—hers much more prodigious than his—so there should have been far less.

Yet, as the rum sloshed in the clear bottle, the level washed well above the top of the label, the meniscus leaving an oily ring reaching into the narrow neck.

He lowered the bottle and glanced at her, but before he could speak, she bit her lip and then gave voice to the same thought that she now projected into his head.

"I know," she whispered through a soft, moist sob. "I drank it dry hours before you arrived." She blinked and a tear separated itself from her eyelash. "Now it's full again—for the third time."

He shook his head, suddenly realizing that her thoughts were now his and his hers. The synchronicity was instantly back and this time the current flowed both directions.

As his mouth formed his next words, she interrupted, thinking her response at him:

::You don't feel drunk, either? Not even buzzed.::

He shook his head.

She smiled as his thoughts flooded her mind. She thought a calm, soft reply.

::Not so fast, let it happen naturally.::

He frowned, and then she responded verbally to his continued flurry of thoughts.

"No, you're right, we're certainly not in Kansas anymore."

Seven

Investment and Return

Alex ran.

She ran with desire and conviction, an irrepressible need *not* to fail. Her strides long, the swing of her arms sweeping powerfully. She ran, but not *away*.

Never away.

She ran *forward*, yet never toward. Toward seemed to imply passive direction. To move toward something meant gaining without arriving; and she needed to feel accomplishment with each run. Whether it was for the mindless escape from the banalities of the day, or the catharsis of a cardiovascular bludgeoning, she committed herself to at least five miles a day.

So she ran.

Actually, she rolled.

Yet, she attacked the winding asphalt trail with the same zeal she applied in her younger days, before the orthopedic guy in Winter Haven made her promise to trade her Nike Decathletes for a pair of in-line skates. Apparently, whatever cartilage was left inside the narrow recesses of her left knee resembled a partially chewed and then regurgitated sliver of Alpine Lace Baby Swiss cheese.

She got the message and reluctantly invested in a pair of high-end lightweight roller-blades; giving up the punishing runs. After only a few minor spills and one major drama involving a bicycle and the right-of-way rules as she understood them, she was racing through the dense forest of Black Pines Trails.

She still thought of her daily exercise as running, and maintained the same arduous approach as her previous workouts. Once she had mastered the subtle differences in balance and coordination, she made no distinction between the two activities. In her mind, she pumped her legs and arms as if she were sprinting competition laps.

So, *yes*. She ran.

Her breath came in deep, controlled tides, matching the steady click and hum of the wheels against the pavement as she swept each leg out and back, pulling herself along the trail with easy effort.

A thin fog had settled into the shallow valleys where the trail dipped and then gradually rose again into the dense woods, frosting the low shrubs in smoky hazy and dressing the taller trees in skirts of moist lace.

Droplets of dewy fog condensed on her face, polishing her high cheeks to a glistening sheen. Her hair, now longer than she ever previously wore it, trailed behind her in a bouncing ponytail. She rose from a sprinters crouch and stretched to her full height, hands on her hips as she coasted toward the square iron railing of the trestle bridge that spanned the torturous waters of the Big Brush River.

Alex glided along the trestle walkway, gradually decelerating as she approached the threshold of the bridge. A blue and yellow butterfly flitted and tumbled alongside her— crossing in front, twirling to the side, looping overhead and behind, and then back across her front. She allowed her lips to part in a easy smile as she watched the aerial display.

Then, like the flicker of a summer mirage hovering over a hot deserted road, the grainy black and white picture caught her eye. The icy itch of recollection scratched ragged talons along her spine.

Her smile wavered for a moment before the desperate block-lettered printing screamed out at her from the handmade sign, slamming her brain with the recoil of a shotgun fired from the deep past. She caught her breath and swerved to a squeaky halt in front of one of the thick iron upright supports for the trestle bridge railing.

There, tacked to the rusty flat metal with frayed black duct tape, was a standard sheet of heavy bond white paper bearing the computer printed likeness of a young girl. In the photo she was smiling sideways—almost slyly—and her eyes sparkled even in the faded colorless reprint. She wore her hair in a braided pony-tail.

The lettering above the photo was obvious and painfully cliché:

Have U Seen This Girl?

But, the text below dripped with sad finality:

> *Daphne Jorgensen*
> *Age 6*
> *Missing since Nov. 12, 2007*
> *Innocent, curious and trusting... my little treasure is gone but never forgotten!! Daphne is an asthmatic. If you know ANYTHING about her whereabouts, please call. If you have her, please care for her.*

The bottom edge of the sheet of paper had many perforated little rectangles with two phone numbers neatly printed on them. A few in the middle had been torn off, leaving a ragged semi-toothed grin flapping in the slight breeze.

The knot in her gut loosened as she swallowed her previous breath.

Christ, when will it ever end?

She clenched her jaw and leaned into her opening stride as she pulled herself away and down the narrow planks of the bridge. She crossed slowly, stiffly sliding from left to right, staring over the side of the railing at the foamy rapids below. The soft snore of the river helped her focus on squelching the mix of anger and despair that wanted to push up from deep within.

Her eyes remained dry, yet violent emotions threatened to break like a storm brewing on the near horizon. She recalled, all too vividly, the desperate handmade notices she had constructed during the weeks following Cora's disappearance.

As she approached the other side of the bridge, she noticed another sheet of paper fluttering in the steady breeze at the base of the railing support on the far side. She closed the distance, knowing full well that it would be another copy of the same missing child notice.

When she was near, she crouched to pick it up, intent on reaffixing it to the metal of the railing upright. She reached for the paper, which she could now see was half-torn down the middle, and snagged it by the corner between her index and middle finger.

When she turned it over, she was shocked and instantly enraged to see that someone had thoughtlessly defaced the little girl's image with graffiti. Her face now sported crudely drawn Groucho Marx glasses and nose, and many of her teeth were blackened out. A huge cartoon penis thrust up from the bottom corner of the page and prodded at the corner of the little girl's mouth.

Alex bitterly crumpled the grotesque ad and threw it with all of her might over the side of the bridge. The wadded paper bounced down the steep muddy bank of the river, lit on the dark rolling waters with a series of soft ripples and was carried swiftly and silently down current.

Alex pulled away from the railing, sprint-skating aggressively down the winding path, strenuously pumping arms and legs that trembled from the effort. Bitter tears trailed across her cheeks as she sliced through the cool morning air. Her breath came in hitches and her heart spasmed, wrought with emotion and anger.

Memories flooded her mind as she climbed the steady rise toward the back end of the park; each dull click of the skate wheels matched her racing pulse. The images and emotions unraveled with the energy of fever-induced nightmares, uncontrolled and violently vivid.

She strode purposely forward as her mind involuntarily fell back...

David. Cora. The poisons of the past...

~ * ~

"Jee. Zus. Christ!" she bellowed as the latest contraction seized hold of her pelvis.

"Easy, now. Keep breathing. You're doing great!"

Alex glared sideways at the OB nurse from beneath wiry wet bangs that hung in her face like storm ravaged Spanish moss.

The young nurse continued to smile, gripping Alex's shoulders in firm support as she curled forward on the side of the bed.

"Shut up, Deb," Alex breathed vehemently. "You ever done this?"

"Twice. And if I recall, you did my second epidural."

Deb smiled reassuringly and adjusted her grip on Alex's shoulders, assisting her into a tighter curl.

"Oh," Alex huffed. Her stringy locks swung in her face and she visibly relaxed as the intensity of the contraction began to fade. "Sorry."

"No worries, Hon."

"All right, you two," the anesthesiologist chided over Alex's shoulder. "Hold still while the Master completes his finest work."

Both women chuffed, mockingly indignant.

Dr. Richard Linc glanced up from his work, eyes wide above his mask, hands frozen with an epidural needle poised and ready.

"Would you like me to continue?" He scolded.

Deb smiled.

With her head bent forward, leaning into Deb's shoulder, Alex could not see either of the two but sensed their levity at her expense.

"Yes, please," she pleaded softly.

"I mean, I could wait for you to..."

"No... Dammit!" Alex hissed through clenched teeth as another contraction hammered at her.

Deb raised her brow, still smiling, and Richard nodded as he deftly slid the needle into Alex's lumbar spine.

Minutes later he secured the thin catheter to Alex's back with clear Tegaderm and long strips of tape.

"Voila!" He exclaimed, popping off his gloves with dramatic flourish.

Deb assisted Alex back into the bed, gathering the monitor cords and IV tubing that had fallen during positioning for the epidural placement. Alex's face was flushed and moist, her hair mussed and wild. She sighed heavily then smiled at Richard as she settled back into the mountain of pillows behind her.

"Thank you, Rich."

He blushed and then shrugged.

"My pleasure, little one." He began busily collecting the trash from his procedure tray.

Previously heavy and charged, the atmosphere of the room now felt lighter, even cooler. Alex closed her eyes and rode out the pressure of the next contraction with a smile on her face.

No pain, she thought to herself. *Only pressure. Marvelous.*

She began to absently scratch at her neck and across her chest. Deb lightly seized her hand as she reorganized the cords and monitor belts around Alex's abdomen.

"That'll only make it worse, remember?" Deb reminded.

Right, she recalled. *The fentanyl.*

"I'll give you some Nubain for the itch," Richard added as he tossed the sharps into a red plastic barrel.

"This is amazing," Alex marveled.

Deb grinned and began charting in quick broad strokes. "Yeah, and just think," she added. "Now you can tell your patients first-hand what the experience is like."

"Testify, sister!" Richard joked.

He now stood at the side of the bed and clasped Alex's hand in his cool dry grip. His fingers were long and nearly engulfed her entire hand to the wrist. He leaned closer and whispered: "Dave's outside... you want me to send him in?"

Alex smiled and nodded toward Deb.

"It's okay, Rich. Deb knows."

Deb winked and then raised a crooked brow.

"Guilty of conspiring to commit a conspiracy." She threw a weak salute with her pen and then went about her tasks within the birthing room.

From the time Alex chose to carry the baby to term, she had kept the identity of the father a closely guarded secret. Having a torrid affair with the chief orthopedic resident was one thing, but to get knocked up was something entirely different. They were both single, so it wasn't as if they had committed some unpardonable sin; it was just that the politics of the hospital—and surgical services in particular—made it difficult for them to carry on any semblance of a normal relationship.

And, the fact that Alex was a student at the time of conception really complicated things. They had been dating covertly for nearly two months before she suspected her pregnancy. She literally had two weeks left in her own residency when the little plastic strip turned blue.

Twice.

She resisted telling David the news initially, both out of fear for his stature as a senior surgical resident as well as her own indecision about what to do. Abortion was never an option, and adoption made no sense to her, even though she knew the programs within the city were excellent at placing unwanted babies.

The surge of commitment had swelled within her with such surprising intensity that she quickly became aware of her wanting—needing—to have and raise this child. It took her the entire two weeks to decide not only to keep the baby, but to work out a feasible strategy to reveal the news to David without freaking him out or jeopardizing his position.

It was all for naught though, as he figured it out on his own the afternoon she graduated.

While her classmates were tossing back merlots and margaritas, sharing anesthesia war stories; she sipped lemon water and lingered pensively at the periphery of the festivities. David arrived later, having traded his call with a colleague, and immediately questioned her choice of beverage. She weakly countered by feigning illness, but he easily saw through her ruse. In minutes she had confessed all; and since that moment, the strain on their relationship never loosened.

Alex nodded appreciatively and squeezed Richard's hand. He was only one of the few mutual colleagues they shared who knew of their impending parenthood.

"Please, send him in."

Richard nodded and ducked past a partially drawn curtain.

"Thanks again," she hollered after him.

"You're welcome," David's soft baritone answered as he entered the room. He approached the bed like a small boy trying to summon enough courage to ask for a pet crocodile.

"Hey, babe," Alex crooned through a tired smile.

"Hey, you," David responded. He sat on the edge of the bed and took both of her hands in his. He smiled widely as he brought her delicate fingers to his lips and kissed each tip.

Alex closed her eyes and purred.

When he finally spoke, his voice was melodious and full of raw emotion. Alex was shocked to hear the quaver in his whispered words and see the trace of tears welling in his eyes.

"I love you, Lexie."

She closed her eyes tightly and purred again, relishing the purity of the moment. "I'm going to be someone's mom," she whispered back.

Eight

The man coughed politely into his fist, as he was brought up to do. The smoke from the little black portable fire-pit drifted lazily around his face as he stretched his back, cracking a few lower vertebrae while twisting from side to side.

What a day.

He took a long, deliberate sip from the wide mouthed goblet. The heat of the fire had warmed the merlot while the dancing light illuminated the vintage to a blood red.

Not arterial red. He mused. *Venous. Dark and viscous.*

He swirled the wine twice and then watched the rich legs run down the curved surface of the crystal. A plump Honey Crisp apple sat on the low wicker table in front of him and when he reached lazily for the fruit, he nearly knocked over the wine bottle. Raising the apple to his mouth, he snapped off a wedge with his large front teeth. The spray of juice flecked the wine glass. As he chewed, he placed the apple down and then reached for a thick slice of cheddar from the stack fanned out across the white plate like mini-playing cards.

Reclining in the *chaise-longue,* he nibbled on the cheese between sips of Yellow Tail. The sun was falling into the trees and the air was chill. After a few minutes, he leaned over the small arm rest and, with a grunt of effort, snagged a quartered log from the modest pile. He poked the fire with the wedge of oak, stirring up a flurry of sparks that twisted into the darkening sky. He carefully placed the log on the fire and then settled back into his chair.

After two more bites of apple, he contemplated the core and then tossed it over the side of the deck. Watching the half eaten apple arc through the air, strike the ground and then roll through the crew cut grass, he found himself reflecting back on that one particular day.

Hell of a drop. Even for a grown man. Yet, she had leapt from the top rail like some kind of tiny ponytailed super hero.

And could she run? Boy, howdy!

He smiled, fingering the stem of his wine glass with one hand while gently scratching the tender skin beneath his silk eye-patch.

Yep. One hell of a day, that was.

Today, too, for that matter.

He was sore from all the digging. Though the soil in this region was old riverbed, you had to get down past the loamy layer and into the real tight clay before you could be confident in planting anything.

Anything you didn't particularly want to grow or harvest, that is.

He was exhausted. Nearly as tired as he was from that chase she had led him on a few months back—her last, to be sure.

Yup, bone-assed tired.

But this was nice, out here tonight. Good wine. Great cheese. The memories of her screams.

He wondered about her and her ingenuity. Her *commitment.* She had been very willful and he had to respect that. Smart, too—obviously: Pocketing the Valium tabs in her fat little cheeks and then faking sedation.

Freakin' brilliant, young lady. He had to give her props there.

But respect at what cost? Just that one day had been too close—almost as bad as the Other-Time—and he was getting too old to continue giving that kind of chase.

If she would've made it to the park, then what? Or if someone did amble down that blasted trail...

Little Miss Creativity had settled it; he would be switching from pills to injections. Sure, it would become more difficult for him to acquire his drugs of preference, but not impossible. People always knew other people that could "hook a brotha' up", as they say.

Suddenly, an image of the Other swam back from the past. The one that *did* escape. *She* had been the reason he'd had to pull up stakes and decamp in the middle of the night—from Ohio to Michigan, under cover of darkness.

And of course, before that it had been from Chicago to the Amish country of central Eastern Ohio. But that hadn't been any fault of his reluctant young guest; that had just been a logistical...

Miscalculation.

He had gotten greedy, that's all. Easy enough to forgive. The beach had just seemed like such fertile ground.

Fresh fruit, ripe for the picking. He'd learned since then. Matured. Improved.

He grimaced at the embarrassing memory of the One-That-Got-Away, grabbed the wine glass in a trembling fist and chugged the rest in two full gulps.

Now *that* little fiasco had definitely been too close for comfort. Fortunately, the drugs had probably made her amnestic—unable to recall anything about him or his predilection for the younger, sweeter things in life. But still...

Where did she eventually end up?

Probably with some naïve Amish family and their fourteen kids. She'd blend right in and they wouldn't know her from Mary, Elizabeth or Rebecca until weeks had gone by.

But that had been nearly three years ago...

And of course someone would notice a well-dressed little blond girl in the midst of all the earthy Amish.

Stupid.

What did it matter now?

His eyes watered and the skin of his face began to itch, as if he were allergic to even the idea of failing. Whenever he thought about the One-That-Got-Away, he had this systemic reaction. He supposed it was a symptom of repressed stress from worrying about getting caught.

But he had a plan for that, as well. He was definitely better at this now than when he first started out; but on the off-chance that he might overlook some important detail or failed to react quickly enough to a situation like The-Valium-Faker's elopement, he needed a quick and foolproof out.

He reached into his front pocket and withdrew the two objects. Placing them on the table before him, he studied their molded, curved outlines in the flickering firelight.

He snagged the one on the right—the light blue one—and tossed it into the metal fire pit.

Won't be needing that *one anymore.*

The legitimate albuterol inhaler melted immediately in the blaze—the plastic loosened and oozed around the small cylinder of medication. The pressurized canister exploded within seconds, spraying the deck and him in a shower of sparks and ash.

"Whoa!" He laughed.

Smiling and shaking his head in satisfaction, he brushed the blast debris from his lap.

He reached for the second inhaler and shook it gently.

One or two puffs rendered immediate unconsciousness while preserving respirations. Five puffs would paralyze the diaphragm and accessory muscles required for breathing, while completely blocking the neuronal intervention to the heart.

He wondered what the brain experienced during that time, if it perceived anything at all. He liked to think that he would dream.

He really liked his dreams.

Nine

Alex stood, hesitant and stiff in the center of the hall, staring at the oversized bulletin board across from the auditorium. Banks of narrow metal lockers stretched down both sides of the wide corridor; their gray, green and russet faces scratched, dented or otherwise adorned with penciled and inked graffiti. The hallways of the high school were relatively empty at eight-thirty on a Thursday evening and she pondered the postings in the echoing silence.

Among the announcements for the holiday musical auditions, snowboards for sale, request for Nickleback concert tickets, algebra tutors, Recycling Club recruitments and an obviously unauthorized filthy limerick, was the black and white flier for Daphne Jorgensen who had been missing since November 12, 2007.

Alex took a careful sip from her tall, insulated coffee cup and considered the odds of her revisiting this particular station of her life. First on her skate this afternoon and now here, tacked to the corkboard in the hallway of the high school: the cherubic visage of young Daphne pleaded for closure. The fuzzy reproduction of the little girl's face was smeared as if each passerby over the last year had lightly brushed the page; gently, yet absently stroking her image in hope to either mystically connect or perhaps—and more likely—to ease the guilt of time-lapsed apathy.

If she were a betting person, which she surprisingly wasn't considering her addictive tendencies, Alex would've bet against any occurrence striking such a resonant chord in such a short span of time. Yet, here she was sipping coffee, procrastinating her entrance into an open AA meeting—her first in nearly a year—by reading the cluttered bulletin board outside the cavernous auditorium. She had every intent of continuing into the meeting, even after she saw the Jorgensen flier, but was now instead constructively wasting time.

Her plans had suddenly and quite unexpectedly changed when she saw the lower half of another announcement stapled awkwardly beneath the flier. It had been printed on high quality glossy pink photo paper in a deep blue italicized font. Curiosity won an immediate victory and she flipped up the corner of Daphne's picture to reveal the shiny pink notice in its entirety.

A Throne for each Child lost in His Kingdom. The quote arced across the top of the announcement.

Apparently, there was a support group for parents of missing children that met tonight in the music room one-half hour before the AA meeting was scheduled to begin. Without much conscious debate at all, she decided to blow off the Twelve Step re-run and try for a little clarity, at Miss Jorgensen's insistence.

Alex turned to find the music room as a door opened down the hall. A couple exited; the woman sobbing into her cupped hands, the man hugging her close around the shoulders with one arm as they shuffled toward Alex. Behind them, the door glided closed with a creak. As they passed her on the far side of the hall, the man glanced at Alex for the briefest of moments. His eyes were dark and empty, void of strength. His exhausted gaze expressed the kind of defeat no one is ever prepared for; a look Alex knew well from her own mirror.

She found herself thinking of David, again wondering what had gone through his head when he first learned of his daughter's disappearance. When did he succumb to the inevitable? Did he truly accept Cora's disappearance as eternal? When had he lost hope?

She knew the answers and sighed, not entirely sure if the sudden anger she felt was aimed at David's stoicism or her own waning hopefulness.

She continued toward the music room as a thought rose from the depths of her resolve.

Mothers never let go.

~ * ~

"Mothers never let go," the woman said as Alex snuck through the door. "And that's okay."

The synchronicity of that phrase with her own thoughts struck Alex like a lightning bolt and she froze in silent contemplation with one hand on the edge of the thick door. Heads turned to watch as she entered.

Her wide eyes must've telegraphed her emotions because each and every face warmed to a smile, some even nodded welcome.

"I know that look," remarked the woman whom had been speaking. She stood regally, yet without pride, in front of nearly twenty people seated in a comfortable semi-circle.

"Randy, would you be a dear and show our guest in?" The woman smiled at Alex as an elderly man with wispy white down at his temples and an otherwise bald pate slowly rose. He approached Alex with the unsteady gait of the chronically arthritic, yet his open arms conveyed a gentle strength that kept Alex from bolting back through the door and down the hall.

Fear and trepidation unlike anything since her initial realization that Cora was gone flooded the hollow spaces of her gut in an icy cascade. Nothing could've prepared her for the mystical combination of anxiety and relief she felt as she took in the expressions on the faces of the group before her.

Randy took her by the elbow and gently guided her forward, allowing the heavy door to whisper closed. They glided around an old upright piano and a large kettle drum, weaved through a forest of sheet music stands and by a water-spotted coffee urn; Alex couldn't help but watch her warped and rippling reflection in the dented surface as she passed. Randy noticed her gaze and nodded toward her Styrofoam cup.

"Whatever you got in there is a far cry better than what Emily brews in that old silver bullet." He smiled as a few gentle snickers warmed the room. Randy showed Alex to an aluminum chair next to his and eased her into her seat with practiced grace and natural chivalry.

"It's true, unfortunately," the woman up front remarked with a sad, yet comical nod. "But we've discussed this before, Randy. You know the kind of riff-raff Starbucks would attract." Belly laughs and loose chuckles echoed around the music room.

Alex sat rigidly and glanced about the semi-circle, taking in the faces: young and old, some seated together as obvious couples, others single. The one glaring similarity was their tired, yet honest smiles.

"I'm Emily," the woman introduced herself with a noble nod.

"And I'm Randy, of course." He bowed at the waist. When he straightened, there was an unexpected pain in his eyes that equally shocked and mesmerized Alex. The easy strength was gone, replaced by something that was not quite defeat but more akin to bewilderment. It was, again, a look Alex knew all too well.

She found herself involuntarily reaching for Randy's arm as a brave question began to form on her lips. Before she could formulate the inquiry, he spoke.

"I lost my grandson while at Six Flags amusement park nearly three years ago." Tears welled in the corners of his eyes, yet his voice never wavered. "I haven't seen nor spoken to my son or daughter-in-law since."

He took his seat carefully, silently, then paused for a breath. His voice finally broke as he finished. "And I'm afraid that I won't ever get to see my other grandchildren again."

Alex simply watched, frozen, as Randy silently regained his composure, her hand resting numbly on his arm. He eventually broke her trance when he took her hand in his and gave it a squeeze. She blinked and accepted his sad smile with a soft one of her own. She then sighed and prepared to introduce herself in the same manner; but suddenly, one by one around the circle, folks spoke up:

"...Dan and Megan, our little girl was riding her bike..."

"...the current is strong there, we knew that buying a house on the river had it's risks but we so wanted to be on the water..."

"...brother-in-law was trustworthy, but then the things they found on his computer..."

Alex listened intently to each and every story, out of respect but also as a shared catharsis. She was amazed by the fact that each experience, though certainly different in the details, had a quality of pain and guilt that resonated to her core.

When the circuit was complete, only one of the seated members had yet to share his story with the group. He sat slightly off to one side, his back to Emily and in profile to Alex. He seemed alert, yet was gazing calmly over his shoulder into the empty space at the center of the semi-circle.

Emily had remained standing and when Alex saw that she wasn't waiting for the young man, that perhaps she was opening the circle to Alex, he slowly turned his face to her and smiled. He had the warm, gentle face of an exhausted yet content little boy and his eyes implored Alex with simple and honest empathy. Alex flushed with the heat of recognition; the young man's face, his eyes, held a glimmer of memory that sparked a sudden tension in her chest. Her skin tightened as sweat erupted along her spine. A stifling wave of familiarity swept through her, powerfully; and then dissipated like a breath in the wind. Her back chilled as the sweat evaporated, the sense of déjà vu quickly fading.

Alex gazed slowly around the gathering and saw nothing but calm, patient smiles. She took a breath and closed her eyes.

"Well, my name is Alex." She paused, out of habit, waiting for the automatic 'Hello, Alex' reply that was so annoyingly common in AA and other support groups. She was pleasantly relieved when there was none and actually laughed a little before she continued.

"I'm an alcoholic, and I only mention this—not because I should be down the hall, which I probably should be—but because that's the reason I lost my little girl."

She surprised herself by the lack of tears and felt an immediate rush of guilt at the apparent lapse of emotion. But the wave of remorse ebbed away before it could reach tidal levels; and after a brief pause she continued.

Alex took her time and further surprised herself with her clarity. Her history was concise and powerful and when she was finished, she felt beautifully drained.

Randy gave her a spontaneous hug while the others nodded sincere empathy and murmurs of welcome.

Someone softly cleared their throat and the room grew preternaturally silent. The quiet young man slid his chair to join the group and looked up at the ceiling for a long few seconds. When he cleared his throat a second time, Emily gently took the empty seat next to him. She laid a soft hand on his knee, encouraging him to speak.

"My, my name is Eric," he stammered a bit at first, but then spoke smoothly.

"And I lost my two younger sisters when I was thirteen…"

~ * ~

As the group broke up, there were hardy hugs and full embraces all around. Each member made an effort to reach Alex and expressed their gratitude for her sharing. She was overwhelmed by the unconditional acceptance and acknowledged each blurred blessing with a thankful smile.

Randy was the last to pass her and as he did, he gripped her shoulder and gave a supportive squeeze. They made eye contact: Hers expressing humble thanks; his, modest grace. He then turned to Emily and nodded.

"'Night, Emily."

"G'night Randy."

With a soft smile he exited through the door, allowing it to creep closed behind him, leaving Alex and Emily alone.

Emily moved to clean up the stranded coffee cups and straighten the chairs. Alex hesitated at the threshold, her hand on the door handle. Emily must've noticed, as she turned to Alex with a smile and a knowing sigh.

"Quite a bit to digest all at once, eh?"

Alex nodded and shrugged.

"I could use a hand with that coffee bullet." She gestured toward the stainless steel urn.

Alex dropped her hand from the door lever and walked back into the room. The two women each grasped the urn by thin-hinged handles and lifted it from the low table.

"Bet you didn't expect there to be so many folks that shared in your hell, either?"

"No," Alex replied.

"We all like to think that we're the only ones—that there's some strange honor in suffering in silence—even when we know that's not true." They hefted the container onto a counter and Alex unscrewed the lid as Emily ran cold water from the tap into the sink.

"The problem with self-pity is that it only gets you so far down the road before you become immune to even your own brand of wickedness." Emily guided the urn, tipping the contents into the sink. The dark coffee swirled in the flow of clear water; the grounds layered the bottom of the sink.

"I'm glad you found us, Alex." She looked to Alex with solemn eyes. Alex held her gaze and then nodded.

"Me too."

Together, they completely inverted the urn, allowing the last bit of aromatic liquid to wash down the drain. Emily swept the grounds toward the center of the drain with her hand.

"Tell me about Eric." Alex surprised herself with her directness, but the image of the young man and his vague story haunted her ever since he had spoken.

"Ah, our young Eric," Emily nodded."Well, as you no doubt ascertained on your own, his story is full of holes. But, that doesn't make it any less tragic." Emily turned off the tap and Alex righted the urn and set it aside.

They moved back toward the circle of chairs and began to absently pick up the remaining cups.

"You see," Emily began. "Eric is autistic. Though he is highly functional. He's twenty-four now, which puts the death of his sisters at nearly eleven years ago."

"Death?" Alex questioned. "I thought he said they were lost?"

"They were, technically. Death is loss, no? And to him, he feels completely responsible for their demise." Emily sighed heavily and abruptly took a seat. Alex pulled a chair close and joined her.

"We can all relate to the guilt one feels for the tragedies suffered upon us," Emily explained.

Alex nodded and stared briefly into space, considering her own suffocating guilt.

"I can't imagine the guilt he must endure, emotionally disabled like that," Alex finally remarked. She shook her head sadly.

Emily only narrowed her eyes in response.

"Alex, every town has its dark secrets—the stories everybody wants to remember, but no one's brave enough to repeat.

"Eric's story is this town's own epic." Emily frowned as she spoke.

"At thirteen years old, that boy cowered in the back of a closet while his mother's freak of a boyfriend, crazy from crystal-meth, worked on those two girls and their mother with a power drill."

Alex cringed, swallowing a leak of bile that had crept up from her clenched stomach.

"Fortunately—or not, depending on your point of view— Eric survived. When they found him two days later, he was still curled up on the floor of that closet. I guess the speed-freak was too cranked up to care about where the 'dummy retard' was. He eventually turned the drill on himself and when he couldn't screw up enough courage to push the bit into his head hard enough, he turned to his .45." Emily shuddered. "I suppose Eric had to endure that, as well."

For the next long minute, Emily stared at the floor between her feet. Alex said nothing.

"So, of course," Emily said finally, "he feels responsible. After all, he's autistic not stupid."

Alex sat quietly, the silence between them swelling with anticipation as she pondered Emily's revelation. One thing still bothered her though, and she had to be very careful how she broached the subject.

Alex looked out of the tall window of the music room into the growing evening. Through the slats of the metal blinds, she watched small groups of people walking down the sidewalk from the front entrance of the school. The AA meeting must've just adjourned.

"Emily?"

"Yes?"

"Did Eric ever spend any time in Chicago?" Alex immediately thought of the spookier version of Eric that she was sure she had met in the ER on that long ago night. His prophetic voice echoed in her memory.

It doesn't have to end with your Cora Rose.

Emily narrowed her eyes, pursed her lips and appeared to give her answer some thought before shaking her head slowly.

"No, I don't think so."

"This would've been last October. Maybe November."

Again, careful consideration and then a much more emphatic negative.

"No, Alex. I'm certain. Why?"

"Nothing." Alex sank back into her chair. "It's just that I could've sworn that I've met him before. In Chicago."

"Sorry, hon. But honestly, that would've been impossible. Especially during the time you mentioned."

"Why?"

Emily readjusted her ass on the hard metal chair and then leaned forward a bit.

"Because Eric was in the ICU on a ventilator from Halloween through Thanksgiving last year. Near fatal bout of bacterial meningitis."

Alex stared, dumbfounded. She suddenly felt foolish, both for believing what she thought she experienced could've been real and then for asking for corroboration in the first place.

Yet...

Mothers never let go.

"Was he unconscious the whole time?" The words were out before Alex could filter them and she was instantly ashamed.

Emily blinked twice, mildly surprised, but then answered politely.

"Yes. But for the most part it was pharmacologic."

"Of course," Alex nodded soberly. "I'm sorry." She didn't know why, but the fact that Eric was unconscious at the time made all the difference. It calmed her a bit, made her feel less crazy about thinking what she was thinking.

Then it suddenly dawned on her, something from Emily's own narrative when she shared her history earlier.

"Emily," Alex asked carefully. "You said that you lost your two nieces nearly ten years ago..."

The air between the two women had grown stifling, heavy with Emily's reluctant pause and Alex's knowing inquiry. Emily eventually gave her a sad smile, blinked back tears and slumped against the metal folding chair with a leaden sigh.

"Yes," she answered. Her whispered voice was tight with horrible memory.

"Eric is my nephew. And Rachael and Ashley were my nieces." She pinched her already narrow lips into thin blanched lines, squeezing strength from deep frozen and forgotten shadows.

"My sister—God rest her self-absorbed soul—was never one to make the right decision about anything," Emily explained. "So when she shacked up with 'Psycho Scott' we all simply took it in stride. It was just another in a long line of poor choices.

"Of course, I saw all of the warning signs. But we had been down that road with her so many times in the past that we had grown immune to it." Her voice took on a defensive tone as she tried to explain. Her expression pleaded, more beseeching than desperate, for understanding—or justification. Alex nodded soft empathy and took Emily's hands in her own.

"When I received the call, I remember thinking only one thing," Emily turned to Alex, busy eyes searching for comprehension, compassion.

"That, finally, the wait was over." Emily's voice hitched with sudden and severe emotion.

"I was finally done with worrying about when, where, and how it would happen. It was mercifully finished. The inevitable was no longer looming over us." Emily sniffed back tearful moisture. Alex squeezed her hands and offered a sad smile of reassurance.

"I didn't even realize how selfish that feeling was until I picked up Eric at the hospital and saw that dread vacancy in his eyes."

Emily swallowed, grimacing against the spasm in her throat.

"It wasn't until after I started this group, after many years of counseling and my second degree in psychology, that I was able to even begin to understand the depth of guilt this kind of loss can thrust upon someone."

Emily turned to face Alex, their hands entwined like reunited sisters.

"Eric is special, apart from his autism," she began. "Most individuals with autistic disorders are incapable of empathy. They struggle in trying to relate to abstract human emotions like sorrow, remorse, even humor. Yet, he has a unique understanding about all things related to our shared tragedies—it's as if he's a seasoned elder with some inexplicable firsthand knowledge and the innate ability to quiet the most profound inner turbulence."

Alex tipped her head forward and to the side, a gesture of tentative acceptance, conditional upon further elaboration.

Emily nodded in recognition and continued.

"He *gets* it, Alex—that weird logic of loss and the bizarre balance of cause and effect that passes for universal justice—in such a pragmatic way that I often have to question his abilities to emotionally cope with his own issues.

"But then I see how effectively he ingests and processes everyone's unique experiences. Unlike the typical autistic, he emotes empathy and sympathy in such perfectly measured doses that I sometimes forget he himself has suffered so profoundly." Emily shrugged and wiped her eyes with the back of her arm.

"I don't know how else to explain it; but tonight was the first time that he openly recognized the loss of his own sisters. And when he spoke to you, Alex, that was the first time he spoke of his sisters in the sense that they were irretrievably gone."

Emily shrugged again.

"I used to think he was just some kind of emotional savant, capable of direct human empathy toward others, yet unable to process his own turmoil. I just thought that he was…I don't know… Hiding.

"Then tonight, he shocks me with this easy candor."

Alex nodded soberly and attempted to offer some insight. "Well, that's a good thing, right? I mean, now you know that he has come to terms with it."

Emily hesitated, biting her lower lip. When she spoke her voice quivered, her eyes widened.

"You don't understand, Alex. Eric hasn't spoken a single word in eleven years."

Alex caught her breath in mid-exhale, nearly choking on the expanding vapors. Emily's gaze locked with hers as she testified further.

"Not a single verbal utterance since the speed-freak and the power drill."

~ * ~

"Thanks for taking the time to come over." Emily unlocked the weathered door with a worn key from her jumbled collection, threw a knee into the lower half, torqued the handle and shouldered it open for Alex.

"Well, thank *you* for the invite."

The rich aroma of fresh bold coffee rolled out of the open hallway, blanketing them in a flavorful cloud dense enough to actually taste.

"Hmmm." Alex couldn't help but close her eyes and openly savor the redolent atmosphere.

Emily smiled mischievously. "There's a great little coffee shop downstairs. Blows Starbucks away," she explained as she slipped past Alex to lead her up the narrow stairs.

"I wasn't joking with Randy about Starbucks," Emily's voice echoed down the stairwell as she climbed the risers two at a time. Alex followed, one at time, but as smooth and quick as her skating strides.

"I've been renting the entire second level for years now, but it's the smells that keep me coming back."

Emily stopped in front of a rust-colored six-paneled door as she expertly fingered the next appropriate key from the array strung on the thin chain dangling from the inner strap of her large purse.

Alex glanced about the short hall and landing, noticing that Emily's apartment door was the only one, when a roll of mail bundled with a thick red rubber band caught her eye. She bent down and snatched up the collection of small envelopes and magazines from against the doorjamb.

"Thanks," Emily said.

Alex shrugged.

The door to the apartment opened with a dull vibrating squeak that turned to a groan as a thick throw rug bunched up against the sweep.

"Be it ever so humble," Emily exclaimed.

Alex crossed the threshold into a crisp airy studio that smelled nothing like coffee. Fresh flowers adorned nearly every flat surface, their fragrances mixed and mingled in a pleasantly shifting mélange. The lighting was expertly arranged so that an even buttery glow suffused the room.

"Make yourself at home," Emily offered as she tossed her purse onto a small low table. The keys jangled within from the gentle impact. "I gotta pee."

Alex smiled and walked through the spacious studio, taking in the tasteful interior.

"You can toss the mail on the front table." Emily's voice echoed from the bathroom as the door clicked closed.

Alex meandered back into the tiny foyer and was about to lay the bundled mail on the table next to Emily's purse when the cover of one of the magazines caught her eye. She pulled the rubber band back and unfolded the bundle enough to expose the entire periodical.

On the glossy cover was the image of a woman, her face partially covered by a blue surgical mask, her hair secured within a flowery bouffant cap. The title of the journal was: *AORN*.

Association of Operating Room Nurses.

Alex smiled and placed the mail alongside Emily's purse.

Footsteps followed a muffled flush as Emily strode back into the room drying her hands expertly on a paper towel that she then tossed absently into a wastebasket in the kitchen as she passed.

Alex smiled and nodded. "So, you're an OR nurse?"

Emily paused for a brief moment, then looked back at the wastebasket and smiled.

"That obvious, huh?" She mimicked her hand scrub.

"That and the journal." Alex tipped her head toward the mail on the table.

Emily nodded, then her eyes silently asked the next obvious question.

Alex answered with a shrug, "I'm a CRNA."

"No shit?" Emily folded her arms loosely across her chest.

"None at all," Alex responded.

"Where at?"

"I'm working locum tenens right now,"

"You know, we're looking for another anesthetist at the hospital here in town." Emily offered.

Alex sighed. "I heard. But locums pays so well right now."

"I hear ya'. Well, if you ever get the itch to settle into a full time staff position, let me know. I'll put in a good word for you. I run the asylum over there."

"Thanks." Alex smiled appreciatively.

Emily hesitated a moment, taking Alex in with wide assessing eyes, then smiled with satisfaction.

"Why don't you come on in, have a seat. I'll be right back." Emily stepped back down the hall, leaving Alex to find a seat in the small sitting room. There were four very comfortable looking beanbag cushions nestled into wicker frames. Alex took one at random and sank into the form-fitting nest with a sigh.

"Diet okay?" Emily returned, dangling a frosty plastic bottle of pop in front of Alex. She accepted and swung her chair around on the smooth swivel joint.

"These are fun aren't they?" Emily settled into her own bag-chair and swiveled back and forth.

"Like college." Alex giggled, sipping her cola.

Emily reached behind her chair, withdrew a thick stack of worn and dog-eared composition books. She quickly thumbed through them, eyes searching. When she found what she was looking for she grunted softly and flung three of the booklets onto the gliding ottoman between them.

Emily fluttered her hand over her lap, pantomiming phantom scribbling.

"Page after page, and notebook after notebook of writing—streams of consciousness, really. He can fill volumes by the week. His journals are the stuff of several lifetimes worth of psychological studies. His minutes of the meetings are the most insightful, articulate observations I've ever read."

Emily took a restful breath, calmed herself somewhat, and then continued. "And not once, in all the hundreds of thousands of pages, has he ever mentioned his sisters—or mother, for that matter—in any of his writings.

"And now tonight, two unexpected revelations at once."

Alex merely sat in silence, staring at the three journal booklets lying across the footstool.

"Alex, I don't believe in coincidence. There is something to this, and it relates to you."

Alex took a deep breath and then shifted her gaze out the darkened window into the night beyond. The image of Eric's face coalesced in her mind and once again she realized that she had made a mental comparison between Eric and the mysterious encounter from her recent past.

"I'm sorry, excuse me." Emily answered her vibrating phone.

"Emily McBride speaking."

Alex's vision blurred as she drifted in and out of a self-induced mini-fugue. She remembered the John Doe from her last night on duty in Chicago, his terrified and knowing eyes as he spoke of Cora, the strength and strange wisdom in his shaky voice. Then she recalled the solemn gaze of Eric McBride as he retold his tragedy for the first time in eleven years. As Alex remembered Eric's soft voice, his deep eyes—their similarity to John Doe's—shards of ice slid up her spine.

They had to be the same person. But how?

By the time Emily terminated the phone call, Alex had leaned over, grasped the three journals and was now perusing the writings within, her bottle of soda balanced between her legs, seemingly forgotten.

Ten

The Expedition rocked with each gust of wind. He fiddled with the cover of her phone, flipping it open and closed with his thumb and forefinger. His mind raced, a mixture of memories: the relentless winter temptress wailing outside, the un-empty fifth of rum, the mysterious and cryptic girl and their unexpected and equally unbelievable psychic connection.

He considered the impossible bottle first, because it seemed the easiest and most concrete of the miracles before him. Lying on its side against the carpeted wall of the rear compartment, the bottle of rum rocked slightly with the motion of the car as the winter gale buffeted the SUV.

Although it had tasted remarkably like ethanol distilled from sugar cane ought to taste, the rum had actually carried about as much potency as that of spring water. In fact, the flavor and bite of the drink had faded with time. He had taken three healthy gulps from the clear bottle only minutes after they had climbed in back, draining the level to well below the bottom edge of the label.

Now, as he glanced at the bottle, he knew the truth in his prediction. Even on its side, he could see that the volume of liquid had once again returned, completely refilling the bottle. He felt not the slightest hint of intoxication, yet vividly recalled the mild burn as the great swallows of Jamaican elixir cascaded down his throat.

Feeling a combination of awe and defeated acceptance of what he was coming to view as warped reality, he shook his head weakly. He flipped open the phone and glanced at the tiny glowing screen. His mind instantly jumped to the series of photos.

"You're thinking about the pictures again?" her voice was muffled from beneath the blanket and piles of extra clothes.

She was awake. And reading his mind. Another, and admittedly more disturbing, of the phenomenon that had recently emerged and redefined his experience of a world he thought he understood.

She nuzzled her narrow face from under the warmth of the blanket, slowly opening her eyes against the cold air.

"Wow," she exclaimed softly. "It got cold."

"Car died," he answered.

"How long..."

::...was I asleep?:: She finished the verbal question as a projected thought. The words sprinted through his mind as clearly and eloquently as if she had spoken them aloud.

Annoying spines of ice slid up his back, and his lungs strained against the frozen cage of his chest each time she did that. It came easier for her than him, and she seemed to smoothly transition from spoken word to direct thought without conscience control. Yet he still resisted, often unsuccessfully, as the ability seemed to manifest itself as persistently as puberty or menopause.

Where she had simply accepted the gift—if that's what it was—and embraced it; he struggled with the impossibilities of the phenomenon and was suspicious of both his own awareness and his sanity.

A gift... From whom? And why? Without conscious control of them, his thoughts fell out of his head, disordered and loud.

::Not for you to question,:: she answered silently. Then she spoke aloud in deference to his uneasiness. "Relax, you worry too much." She smiled.

He grimaced, and before he could catch himself, another slurry of random thoughts raced through his mind: *Who is she, where are we and what is with this? Am I in Wonderland?*

"Maybe," she said, again verbally. Then she thought at him, hard. *::We've already gone through this, remember? You don't know who you are or where you came from. Neither do I. We have no names; at least that we can remember. Yet here we are.::*

"For a reason," she concluded, out-loud for emphasis.

He sighed and stared at the screen of the phone hoping vainly for strength and clarity within the solid-state construct.

But there would be none found there.

She rose up on one arm, stretched the sleep from her curled form and folded into a lotus position. She was smiling as she considered his frown.

::Still trying to figure it out?:: she asked in thought.

"Stop doing that," he admonished. "Can't you talk out loud?" He shook his head in frustration.

She smiled.

"Sure, but it's so much easier to just think it. Come on." She slid across the space between them and took both of his hands in hers. "You are going to have to face reality sooner or later."

"Reality?" he cried in astonishment. His voice was loud and cracked with fear. "This," he waved dramatically about the car, "is not reality!" He shook his head to emphasize his point.

She looked outside at the raging and endless winter storm, a soft smile still held her lips in a lovely arc.

"I mean, look." He pointed to the bottle. "If there was any rum in that, it's long gone. Where did it go? And what keeps replacing it?" She causally glanced at the bottle as it rocked back and forth against the carpeted sideboard; her face remained serene.

He flicked a finger against the face of his watch. "What about the time?" He asked, his voice tinged with desperation. "I have no idea what day it is, much less the time.

"Where are we? Who are you?" He looked into her eyes for a second time as he repeated his previous unspoken question and then blinked against rising moisture.

"And what is with this…" He drummed his thumb against his temple three times and then flipped it back and forth between their heads indicating their apparent psychic connection. His eyes were wet and wild with frustration, fear, and defeat.

Two names—images of the ideas of names, really—flashed through his racing mind:

Eric. Alex.

They were meaningless to him at first. But some lingering after-image told him that they were significant at one time. But not now.

Not important.

She squeezed his hands, leaned into his shoulder and remained silent.

The blizzard continued to rage, the snow whipped in an endless dance and the car rocked gently to the music of the wind.

Eleven

After adjusting her pager from audible alarm to vibrate and securing it to her elastic waistband, Alex thumbed her purple iPod into shuffle mode and tucked it neatly into the Velcro pouch strapped to her arm.

She pushed off from the threshold of her wide driveway in three smooth strides and glided down the slight slope of the private road leading from her house to the public trail. The funky pulse of Black-Eyed Peas thrummed from the ear buds as she gently screwed them in place. Coasting on her roller-blades, she picked up speed, controlling her decent with wide graceful arcs as she weaved from shoulder to shoulder. As the entrance to the trail approached she dragged one skate, executed a smooth left-hand turn and then began striding up the narrow trail, arms swimming and legs pumping.

The afternoon sun pressed toward dusk behind her, deep orange light flickered through the low hanging trees lining the winding black asphalt. Her shadow played out before her, long, jagged and flitting as she leaned into her strides. The trail became the opposition and soon she worked herself into a rhythmic aggression, pulling herself along the snaking, twisting path.

Black Eyed Peas gave way to Rob Zombie as she fell into a hypnotic gait. The vibration of the wheels on the soles of her feet and the crisp riffs of rock music set her mind into a groove as naturally as any memory could.

She thought of the past week and the strangeness that surrounded her as it had ended. She reflected on her visit with Emily and the surreal revelation that Eric and her John Doe were somehow inexplicably connected. She recalled the text of Eric's journals, printed in tightly packed angular script, and how the thoughts flowed smoothly, purposefully.

The lengthy entries sketched out in Eric's methodical hand had suggested vague internal musings about theology, philosophy, and physics; but also hinted at a distinct separation from reality. Despite this apparent disconnect, there was a comforting sense of synchronicity to everything.

A familiarity not unlike...

Memories.

~ * ~

Eric had written in a crisp, slanted hand:

> *Time is relative to both the Tyro and the Devices while in the Crease.*
> *And space, infinitely folded.*
> *Today, tomorrow, yesterday means nothing without a point of reference. It is the observer that is important, not the observed. At any given time, in any given space, a conscious decision must be made in order for a specific event to take on any degree of meaning. It is this specific consciousness that defines the universe wholly...*

"This is not the writing of an autistic," Alex had exclaimed upon digesting the first of many pages.

"You're right," Emily answered. "In fact, most autistics cannot grasp the subtleties and abstractions of expression such as figurative speech, humor, metaphor or other nuances. And most struggle with written language altogether. It's called dysgraphia. Yet for whatever reason, Eric has had this savant-like skill since the day we buried his sisters."

"And he never showed this talent previously?"

Emily shook her head.

"Actually, there are many forms of autism," Emily had continued. "And I may have over-simplified earlier. Eric has Aspergers Syndrome. Technically, it's not true autism, but closely related."

"I know that disorder," Alex mused. "But isn't one of the classifications a tendency toward overly verbose one-sided conversations?"

Emily nodded.

"Yet, you said that Eric has been silent for over a decade."

Except when rambling on about things he couldn't possibly know while lying in an ER bed in Chicago when he was supposed to be unconscious somewhere up in Michigan, Alex thought.

Emily nodded again, sullenly.

"Yes," she said. "And until that day, Eric had been a classic study in Aspergers. He would engage total strangers in long-winded dissertations about clocks and watches and sundials. Anything related to time-keeping devices. That was his thing.

"He could even tell you the exact time of day without a clock or watch. Then I think the trauma pushed him into something completely different. Maybe even new.

"Nobody's been able to pin it down." Emily sighed. "And he's been seen by the best." She shrugged.

Alex had continued reading.

Free will is not an illusion. Conscious choice is perhaps the most important aspect to consider when defining the human condition. The truth of the matter is that, although free will persists, it means nothing. Regardless of the causal relations between choices and consequences, each and every single choice has a finite number of consequences and those pathways are well established before any conscious decision is made. All of the possible outcomes for any decision already exist, it is only when they are directly observed that they are realized and become actual.

While outside of the Crease, an individual is like a cell moving through the myriad branches of the arterial tree. At each fork in the path a decision must be made and once made, he continues forth. If he chooses the left branch, that pathway is directly observed and then becomes his reality. That does not make the right branch any less real, just meaningless to that individual.

Within the Crease, however, all possibilities are equally meaningful (or meaningless)—regardless of objective relativity.

Alex shivered, reached for her pop and after a shaky sip, spoke with a ragged edge of fear to her voice. "This is creepy, Emily. I haven't heard shit like this since watching Carl Sagan's "Cosmos" as a kid."

Emily nodded somberly. "I know, and the worst part is that he samples popular metaphysical paradigms and blends them together almost seamlessly: Relativism, Unified Field theories, Quantum physics, String theories, even the dreaded Singularity postulate."

Alex gaped, struggling with the terms.

Emily shook her head dismissively. "Ignore the geek in me. Suffice to say, that I did quite a bit of research after reading these."

"Well, where in the hell did he pick this stuff up? I mean, this would be heavy material for Stephen Hawking, never mind a junior high drop-out with Aspergers." Alex threw her hands up in question.

Emily could only shrug.

Alex closed the first book and opened the third at random.

> *It is while within the Crease that the Tyro will learn from the Devices how to pass from Fold to Fringe and back. That past, present, and future are ultimately meaningless. And although free will exists and decisions are human-dependant catalysts; everything has an exactly balanced opposite. So that darkness is exactly neccessary for light, vacuum is exactly necessary for mass, evil is exactly necessary for good.*
>
> *When these elements are imbalanced, it becomes necessary for corrective intervention. Erinyes prevails and the Thrones ensure that necessary balance is maintained.*

A ghostly shiver crawled up Alex's spine as she re-read that latest entry. When she finally looked up at Emily, the question fell from her lips as a dry whisper. "What is the Crease and who are these entities?"

Emily frowned. "Tyro, Devices, Erinyes, and Thrones?"

Alex nodded slowly, numbly, as she remembered the phrases from her own past.

Find your way into the Crease. Learn from the Devices.

"I've looked them up. They're real. At least from a religious and mythological standpoint. But I can't say for sure what he might've meant in using them. He may have borrowed the terms to describe something indescribable."

"Have you ever asked him?"

"Hmmm." Emily nodded. "He just holds his hand over his heart, looks deeply into my eyes, touches his temples with his fingertips, and then folds his hands back over his heart in solemn prayer. It's frightening." Emily shuddered.

"Okay, so what do *you* think?"

Emily held Alex's gaze with sad intensity. "Are you religious, Alex?"

~ * ~

Alex glided around a gradual curve, leaning into the turn as she scanned ahead for foot traffic. She rose to her full height and reached for the iPod strapped to her arm. She quickly scrolled through the menu, searching both title and artist for song that had become lodged in her memory.

Loosing my Religion. R.E.M.

She didn't have it.

She returned the MP3 player to its Velcro pouch and increased her stride, shaking her head at the memory of the prophetic journals.

Suddenly, ahead of her and to the right of the narrow path a small dark-haired girl struggled with her Razor scooter. Alex deftly swerved as she called out. "Watch it!"

The girl jerked her head around at Alex's warning; her braids flopped against her round cheeks. Her face, partially shadowed by a bright red hoodie, was nearly comical with surprise, yet her eyes held a glint of fear that tore into Alex's heart.

She immediately regretted frightening the girl, and as she soared around the silver Razor she threw up an animated wave and flashed a wide warm smile.

"You're okay, Honey."

The girl smiled back, tentatively, and wiggled two fingers of one hand in a weak return wave. Her mouth held the smile, yet her eyes still vibrated with unrefined fear.

Shit. I really scared her. Then she was around the next turn and on through the darkening forest.

Twelve

The endless winter blasted the Ford as Eric shivered; his struggling mind considered the prophetic photos.

The images were the same but the emotions they elicited were now much different. Though he still didn't recognize the man or the woman in the six digital stills, he sensed that they were important and that somehow all their futures were intertwined.

Holding the phone in his lap, he scrolled through the digital photo gallery watching each of the six images flash onto the small LCD screen:

The man, alone against an opaque background, looking to his right. The woman, crying as she rakes her hands through her long hair. The man again, peering into the camera as if squinting against a flash, his right eye frosted over and blind. The woman, her pale face rigid, eyes flirting with a tacit glare that suggests anger. The man walking away from the camera into a milky haze as he looks over his right shoulder, a shadowy smirk touching the corners of his mouth. And lastly the woman, her eyes closed, face turned to the sky, lips drawn into a loose smile of either relief or acceptance.

"Now you see," she said to him as the wintry gale blew against the side of the car. He raised his eyes to meet her intense gaze. Her voice now had strength—a certain depth of confidence that had not existed before.

He sensed that she had changed, somehow, from the timid melancholy stranger into someone—or something—more sentient; wise from experience.

He turned the phone over in his hands, marveling at the mystery of the six pictures that had appeared on their own. He still couldn't retrieve the date or time from the phone; and, in fact, the power indicator showed that the battery should've been dead. Yet, the phone had chimed, signaling an incoming message and when he flipped open the cover, the images downloaded automatically from thin air.

There was no originating sender identification and once the images were loaded, none of the phone's other functions were operational. Only the six pictures and the ability to scroll through them remained.

He shook his head and sighed. As his next thought developed, she plucked it easily from his mind and began to smile.

::*I don't know the man,*:: she thought at him. ::*Although I've seen him before; he seems unfamiliar. But...I sense pure evil in him.*::

He nodded slowly, in absolute agreement as he stared at the image of the man with the long facial scar and the dead eye.

::*And the woman?*:: he asked silently.

She smiled sadly, tears welling in the corners of her eyes. ::*I thought that would've been obvious by now,*:: she answered.

He looked up from the small screen and caught her gazing longingly at the image of the young woman crying. When she raised her eyes to meet his, the recognition stunned him like an electric shock. The similarities were subtle but once established, striking and unmistakable.

He opened his mouth to speak but she snagged the thought from him before he could bring it to voice.

"In some ways, it seems so long since that day—a day that hasn't happened yet," She whispered aloud, "Then again..."

::Time is relative,:: he answered in thought.

She nodded slowly, her response slid into his brain easily. Warmly.

::Especially here.::

His gaze had locked onto the bottle of faux rum, rocking gently on its side. He stared, trancelike, watching the clear liquid agitate within the glass as the wind whipped against the car. He felt impossibly contrary—both grounded and disjointed—and as his focus intensified, the perception of his small frigid world began to blur. He wanted to blink, to clear his vision, but could only stare.

The bottle began to fade, seeming to melt into the carpet of the car's sidewall, and then the sidewall itself began to loose color and substance. He imagined—or thought he imagined— that the whole car was actually loosing mass and that if he concentrated, he could see the dancing flakes of snow through the solid body of the vehicle. With some effort he broke his trancelike state and tore his eyes from the empty space where the bottle had once lain.

He quickly scanned his close surroundings and immediately realized that what he initially perceived as blurred or double vision was, in fact, universal dissimulation.

The bottle, the car—everything but the snow and the dark night—was fading; growing steadily more opaque; waxing toward complete translucency.

Everything except her.

And him.

They remained seated, legs crossed and facing one another, incomprehensibly floating atop a great swell of snow as the Ford Expedition and all that made it such vanished silently and completely.

Fear stormed his consciousness as their bodies settled onto the soft snow without so much as a crunch. Unprotected now from the elements, the wind bit at his cheeks and raked his hair; and for a second he was terrified that she too would begin to fade, then vanish, leaving him alone to die in the frigid blizzard.

But the fear quickly passed and she took both of his hands and smiled. Her face was open and nearly childlike, yet her eyes remained deep, hooded by ancient wisdom and intense with a strength and conviction that seared with cosmic justice. Her gaze held his, commanding and irresistible.

The primal appetites of fear, loneliness and confusion left him in an effortless sigh. Her ancient memories flooded his consciousness, pouring into that remaining chasm for a brief moment—a cosmic blink—and then vanished forever.

He was again awash with emptiness as raw as he could ever have imagined. The void within felt abysmal, but not alarming. Instead, he felt calm and pure; and the vacuum swelled with what he could only describe as innocence—purity.

She smiled expansively, the emotion now spreading to her eyes, softening the crystalline intensity as they sparkled anew with clarity and understanding.

::Now,:: she exclaimed, the thought exploding pleasantly in his head. *::I think you get it!::*

He intended to shrug, and his shoulders seemed to comply, yet his response flashed effortlessly from his mind to hers at the speed of thought.

::Do I?::

She blinked and nodded in affirmation then slowly, gently, turned her back to him, releasing his left hand as she repositioned herself kneeling in the snow.

He hadn't noticed until he saw the smoothness of her bare back, and was unsure when the change had occurred, but she was now completely naked. She left no impression in the snow where her body made contact, but instead seemed to rest weightlessly atop the unbroken surface.

As she kneeled before him, her back turned, she thought and he received a clear command.

::We haven't much time.::

With that, he completely understood her intent and knew what was expected. He glanced down at his own freshly naked form and smiled with new, growing confidence. He rose to his heels and turned on his haunches until they were crouched together atop the unfractured surface of the snow, back to back.

They reached behind themselves and clasped hands as they both turned their faces to the open sky. They shared a final thought as their mind-voices sang in unison one last time before the transformation was completed.

He/She cried-laughed-gasped at the wonder of the Truth born before Them.

Tyro and Device.

The white crystalline flakes spun out of the blackness, spiraling down from the eternal void of space, racing past and then condensing upon Them. The velocity of the white flecks increased until they were no longer individual snowflakes but streaks of pearly coherent light flashing past and through Them. The sense of speed was so incredible that it was impossible to separate Their motion from that of the Universe.

Snowflakes became stars as the cosmos expanded. Each distant sun winked and sparkled as the whiteness of the snowstorm fell away, replaced by the atramentous blizzard of astral infinity. Eons folded into fractions of nanoseconds and the stars collapsed, then swelled to the size of atoms, each sun a nucleus with clouds of electrons for planets.

They were, in the same instant, as enormous as the suns and their planets, and as small as the simplest elementary particle. They were both galactic and sub-atomic, negative and positive, dark and light, with mass and without.

They were before life and after death, born of the cosmos, and mated with the stuff that falls between Time.

They now tread with orders of Angels too numerous to account; and too pure to comprehend.

They had become *Necessary*.

Thirteen

Reaching the small park, Alex slowly glided around the cul-de-sac marking the end of the trail. After completing one circuit, she jumped the small curb and skated through the empty parking lot. As she spiraled toward the middle of the lot, she casually swerved between the faded yellow lines marking the narrow parking spaces. Her mind drifted between Emily's revelations and her last night on duty back in Chicago.

She sensed a connection, the root of which eluded her in a nagging, almost teasing way. The harder she concentrated on the puzzle, the more transparent any similarities became, yet when she allowed the memories to simply evolve on their own their shared history seemed natural. Even logical.

Eric and the strange woman from the ICU had been trying to tell her something. Despite being polar opposites, they had both been intensely confident in exercising the completion of their task—almost insistent. Yet the importance of each of their messages seemed magnified only by their overall serenity. The strangeness of their similarities, intermingled with their distracting differences, caused her heart to chill and her throat to tighten with an anticipatory tickle. There was no question, in Alex's mind, that the two enigmatic messengers were related; and the more she thought about it, the more she tended to view them as a necessary duality.

Good and Evil.

Dark and Light.

The setting sun steadily waned from mango orange to deep plum red as the solar disk swelled toward the horizon. She coasted to a stop at the foot of the curb and paused there to watch the glassy crests of small waves dance over the hidden rocks in the river bed.

The filtered light of dusk dyed the flowing waters various shades of brilliant fire as the moderate rapids churned and gurgled. The frothy surface held the vibrant plumage of the sunset; each irregular wave sparkled and twinkled with feathers of crimson, amber and gold. Just beneath the flashes of reflected sunset, she knew with dread certainty that the river's dark current churned unseen along the shadowed bottom, sucking rocks, plants, fish, crab and river clams down-stream in a ceaseless, unforgiving pull.

She absorbed the tranquil scene with a painful sense of powerless awe and eerie reverence. The reverberant rush of the rapids mesmerized Alex—the continuous static of flowing water across rocks, worn smooth over time by trillions of gallons a day.

So much of life was like the river: the endless, unyielding course of time dragging the debris of the past downstream, bouncing and jostling over rock and earth, sometimes allowing flow through a path of lesser resistance, and sometimes not. Where the pass became treacherous, the river, like life, sang a boisterous song. When easier avenues opened, the flow increased and yet, the river became quiet.

But in the dark depths, beneath the smooth waters of quieter passage, the insistent unforgiving pull of the current can sweep away entire portions of your life.

And how difficult it was to travel up-stream against the current of time. Even if you got out of the river and walked along the bank back to your staring point, the water you observed then was not the same river you traveled previously. She reflected on the silt of her own past, the debris of life that churned along the bottom of her internal river. She saddened at the thought of lost time, the missed opportunities, the vacuum where pleasant memories should swell to fill the empty void.

Of course, she thought of Cora.

Before the tears could start she forced herself to stay grounded in the present. She focused on her successful anesthesia career, her new job and home, her sober second chance at a clean future.

Despite the hungry, nagging ghosts dwelling in her closet, things could be worse. She scolded herself silently for allowing the weakness of self-pity to surface and tried to reorganize her thoughts. But she was repeatedly distracted by the recollection of the two homeless messengers that, despite rational reasoning, most definitely were trying to tell her something. One seemingly dark and the other, frighteningly hopeful.

The Crease.

Find a way into the Crease.

Christ, I need to get to a frigging meeting.

She hadn't been to an AA meeting since she moved north—nearly five months—for no better reason than sheer laziness at first; and then, of course, her preoccupation with Emily's support group. She hadn't religiously attended before, only the occasional meeting when life's stressors overwhelmed her and temptation set in. In fact, that was one of the reasons she shied away from them. The *Religion.*

While Alex had been baptized and raised Catholic, she was by no means an active participant of any specific church and like many of her professional-student colleagues, had stopped attending altogether during residency. Getting back into the swing of Sunday morning worship never rose any higher on her To-Do list than the bottom tier of a category entitled Foggy Childhood Traditions That Would Be Nice To Reestablish.

That didn't mean that Alex was without spirituality, only that she had more than her share of issues with the popularity of institutionalized religions in general and the concept of an all-benevolent God in specific. Far too much had transpired in her life for her to buy into blind faith.

Which brought her right back to her missing daughter. How a God of Love could allow that to happen to a mother and daughter—and in fairness to David, a father—was a question for the ages. And what of all the other missing, abused and murdered innocents? How is that justified in the dogma?

How could God allow even the *concept* of filicide to exist?

Alex still felt convinced that if God—or a Higher Power, as the Friends of Bill in AA liked to refer to the deity—existed; that entity was far too mysterious and, quite honestly, far too selfish in Its motivations for her to allow herself to unconditionally entrust to Its will. She was sick of the blathering zealots and their feeble attempts to console her grief with statements that claimed that 'things happened for a reason', or that 'God works in mysterious ways'.

Or her favorite, *God Was Calling Cora Home.*

Alex knew none of these explained away the biting facts: She had fucked up, plain and simple. She had gotten drunk at the beach, passed out, and lost her baby girl. Abducted or drowned, she figured—at times hoping for the former, while at others praying for the last.

Prayer.

Now, there was another colossal waste of time and energy.

With a heavy, angry sigh, Alex pushed off from the curb, coasting away from the river vista as the sun dipped below the tree-lined horizon and the sky bled violet in the east.

If God did exist—and surprisingly, Alex really didn't doubt it, even though she would never *worship* such a being—and He did have a hand in Cora's disappearance, then He allowed it to happen for no other reason than that Alex was simply not worthy to continue caring for such innocence.

Alex had initially shouldered the guilt and blame out of self-flagellation over her weakness for the rancid drink, but soon graduated to full blown martyrdom when she realized that besides drinking like a Viking at nearly ever opportunity, she simply had made bad decisions all-around. From choosing to have an affair with a prominent up-and-coming surgeon to rearing his child; she had always allowed her selfish appetites, her nccd for acceptance and false self-esteem to rule her life.

The only good, or at least beneficially positive decision she made was to attend anesthesia school and see it through to the end.

And refusing to cave to David's pleas to get an abortion.

Alex increased her strides, pumping her arms and sliding her legs wide; sweeping along the asphalt trail as it curved in and out of the forest, chasing the wide river. An occasional flicker of fireflies dotted the air over the high prairie grass as the sky deepened from cobalt to bruised purple.

She had quit drinking because of the loss, sure. But she stayed sober for herself; at least that was what her sponsor told her she should think. Though at times, Alex had to admit that the only reason she didn't reach for the booze was out of pure challenge. She didn't like to lose and wasn't about to fall to something so banal as alcohol.

And God hadn't helped her achieve that level of self-control, either. No, that distinction went to Sandy, her sponsor. Sandy had been there when they told her that they were calling off the search for Cora and that, though the case would remain open, it would be what the authorities called a Cold Case. A mystery. Unsolvable without further clues.

Sandy had also been there for the memorial service (Ah-ah... *remembrance* service), arranged and insisted upon by David so that *he* could have closure and move on. Sandy had held Alex like a shattered toy many nights that winter. She'd never said a word, just cradled Alex in her thick arms, caressed her brow and rocked her to sleep until the dreams would wake her in hysterics.

Fellow Twelve-Steppers had admonished Alex for her refusal to accept God's handiwork in her recovery, claiming that it was God's will that Alex found them and that even Sandy was an agent of God's desire to help Alex stay healthy and sober. Sandy, however, would simply sit silently, an embarrassed smile touching the corners of her eyes as she sipped cheap coffee from a short Styrofoam cup. She understood Alex like they couldn't.

Like even God couldn't.

Alex had continued to attend meetings because of Sandy and when the older matron died unexpectedly from a massive heart attack, Alex—alone—had buried her. Sandy had no family.

Alex didn't recall God being anywhere around for that little event either.

So no, Alex didn't lend a whole lot of credence to the Higher Power argument. She was clean and sober now because she chose that path and if she went to a meeting it was not because the Lord compelled her to do so. She attended for the memory of her friend Sandy and if she took anything home with her afterwards it was simply the shared struggle and rare wisdom of fellow alcoholics.

The program *was* good, however, and Alex wasn't so much of cynic as not to see that many people benefited from Alcoholics Anonymous and its offspring support groups. She had issues with some of the tenets, true; and even though the hardcore elders may have frowned upon her reluctance, they always accepted her as a sister of the Weakness.

To each their own, and in varying degrees.

Alex rose from a crouch as she coasted out of a curve and stretched her back, slowing her pace, gently crossing one skate over the other.

She resolved to step into the next open AA meeting at the high school just to reestablish some commonality in her new life and also hoped that in this two-traffic-light rural burg, no one aside from Emily would recognize her from the hospital. She didn't hold a lot faith in the anonymity portion of the group's credo, either. Small town talk was still a frustrating mystery to her.

As she rounded the next curve, a flash of metal along the edge of the path caught her eye. She slowed, approaching the object.

A silver Razor scooter.

The silver Razor scooter—she was instantly sure—that belonged to the little girl she passed not thirty minutes before. Alex's throat suddenly spasmed with fear as she dragged her left skate behind the right, rubbing silently to a halt.

Where's the girl? A familiar, panicky voice screamed inside her head. She felt the chill of a distant on-coming storm. Tactile memories of the bitter cold of crashing waves ran through her mind, a freezing knife sliced up the back of her neck. The empty terror of loss flooded her soul—the piercing memory of the afternoon she lost Cora.

Her heart stopped, then jumped with an icy clang. She stared at the silver metal of the scooter, the remaining light of the approaching evening reflected dully in the polished tubular surfaces. For a brief moment, she was terrified to look anywhere but down. She feared what she may find.

Then a hollow thud followed by a deep, soft voice startled her into action. She whirled toward the sound. It came from across a narrow strip of sparse prairie grass covering the gradually descending bank of the river.

Without thinking, she stepped off the path and into the knee-high grass. Crouching stealthily and balanced on the narrow wheels of her in-line skates, she walked deeper into the swaying stalks of pale grass. Her ankles strained against turning under as she side-stepped across the uneven ground, the wheels of her skates rolling and dragging shallow gouges into the soft soil.

She heard another hollow sound, followed by a second and then a low grunt. She gently parted the stalks of grass and peered ahead. She then worked toward the edge of the river, the incline of the bank becoming steeper as she crept forward.

Beneath the mocking whisper of the river, she detected something that altered the uniformity of the otherwise undisturbed current. The presence of something artificial in the water was confirmed by a clumsy sounding splash and then a whispered—or mumbled—curse.

She would be able to see the rolling waters of the river when she parted the next clump of grass plants, and as she reached out her lungs tightened with anticipatory fear. Her heart drummed staccato beats against the delicate membrane of her inner ear and small red spots danced behind her eyes— the adrenaline of a sympathetic rush. She wanted to take a deep breath and count to ten, relax and regroup; but her nerves rebelled and resisted. She held her breath instead.

Alex spread the last stand of thin grass stalks with both hands. A twin-seated kayak listed to its port side on the muddy bank of the river. The bow of the narrow watercraft rocked in the mud of the shore, the small keel carved uneven grooves in the black moist earth as the stern bobbed in the water. The force of the current rocked the kayak from side to side and with each dip to the port side, Alex could see into the shallow bottom of the vessel.

Glimpses of a red hoodie. A small white and purple tennis shoe with friendship beads strung onto the laces. Dirty denim jeans. The clumped articles of clothing were small, meant for a child. But it wasn't until she noticed the two shocks of braided hair jutting from under the hoodie that she realized the clothes actually enshrouded the girl's body.

Alex rose from her crouched position and turned sideways to negotiate the slippery bank in her skates. She had made three steps, sliding a little as she dug the edges of the wheels into the soft mud, before his voice startled her.

"Hey!"

She pin wheeled her arms to catch her balance as she abruptly turned toward the deep voice.

He stood above her and to the right, on the high edge of the bank. His hair was long and nappy, small ratty tails framed his scarred face. His eyes—*eye*—narrow, uneven and squinting; seething and hot with aggression. That one eye looked straight at her, a deep neon blue; while the other gazed off to the side, frozen askew and opaque with a thick smoky cataract. He blinked, but only the good eyelid moved. A faded jagged scar ran the full length of his cheek from the corner of his diseased eye to his neck, ending in a rough knot of bubbled, reddened skin. The angry burn scar stretched the skin of his face tight on that side and then disappeared under the collar of a well-worn Carhartt coat.

He clenched his mouth, lips white against his teeth and rigidly set jaw. With the ferocity of a large Black bear swatting at cornered prey, he swung the long wooden oar fully and completely.

Edge first, it caught Alex solidly across the side of the head. Lightning exploded in her mind as the flash of pain instantly blinded her. She fell like a fly hit by a windshield. One thought danced on the periphery of her consciousness a fraction of a second before she died.

Mothers never let go.

Fourteen

She must've died... right?

That blow had to have knocked her clean to Heaven.

And a wintry Heaven at that.

Either that, she thought wistfully, or the Cubs had finally won the World Series and she was actually waking up in Hell where, according to popular sports prophecy, the temperature would steadily drop. Thick, cottony snow fell and swirled in cords and curtains around her as she rose to her feet. She was dressed in thin exercise gear—tight shorts and two layered tank tops—and sensed the cold, but was not at all bothered by the discomfort.

That was odd.

All around her was empty, eternal whiteness, fuzzy with thick snowfall. The wind *seemed* to howl, but the air was actually still and soundless.

She gazed down at her body, her fingers caressed the smooth Spandex-like material of the Under Armor gear and she struggled for a moment to place herself. She hadn't a clue who—or where she was. Yet, she had vague memories of beaches, parties, hospitals, faces without names and places without meaning. The glut of disjointed images ran easily through her mind, strange and foreign, yet not at all disorienting.

Squinting against the sting of blown ice crystals as she peered into the distance, she turned in a full circle, scanning for...

What?

She should be concerned, even fearful of her condition—her amnesia. But instead, she was calm, almost serene.

Instinctively, she stuck her tongue out to catch a snowflake. A fat one landed and melted instantly. She turned her face up to the sky and allowed the flakes to accumulate. Varying in size and shape, they lit upon her skin; some bounced off while others stuck for a second and then melted. Only the few that clung to her eyelashes and brows remained intact. That fact seemed important all of the sudden, though she could not sense why. She blinked and the flakes scattered, continuing their fall to the ground.

A squawking bleat shattered the silence, startling her. She spun around and faced into the blowing blizzard, listening intently to the chirps and warbles of the disturbance. She recognized the sound, found it remotely familiar; yet could not place it until, as she squinted into the whiteout, she could barely discern the blurry shape of a car in the distance.

Car alarm, she realized.

Without hesitation and drawn—or pushed—toward the car by some unseen force, she trudged through the snow. She lowered her head into the prevailing wind, which only now had grown a siren-like voice, and took step after unbalanced step.

As she picked up her feet, she realized that she wore only socks—oversized white athletic crews that bunched up at the ankle. She paused and turned to look back at the point from which she started. Her tracks were already beginning to fill with drifting snow; but there, ten feet behind her were a pair of in-line skates resting on their sides, laces curled in the white powder.

She wanted to marvel at this weirdness, rationalize whatever reasons she may have had to not only wear inappropriate footgear out in a blizzard but then to abandon that for mere stockinged feet. She wanted to spend some time thinking about that puzzle, but it suddenly didn't seem as important as it had only a moment before. Besides, her feet were not cold in the least.

Strange.

She continued to walk and the alarm grew in volume as she approached.

~ * ~

"Hello?"

She swiped a clean circle in the accumulated snow and then gently rapped on the window with two bare knuckles. Standing on her toes, she leaned forward, her small nose touching the cold glass, trying to peer into the blackness of the Ford's interior. Her breath fogged the glass, so she wiped the surface clean again and tapped the glass harder.

"Hell—o?" She drew out the second syllable musically.

She reached out to try the door handle. Her fingers curled under the latch just as the window wound down with a loud mechanical whine.

"Oh..." Startled, she jumped.

A cloud of breath plumed from the partially opened window.

"Hi. Yeah, I'm sorry," a groggy male voice said. "Caught me sleeping."

The air in front of her danced and shimmered in turbulent waves as the warmth from the passenger compartment swirled about her head. The moment she felt the heat wave she began to take notice of the cold.

She had taken a step back initially, but now leaned forward in effort to see the man inside. His features remained in shadow yet his hand moved from the steering wheel, reached through the window and caught a few fat flakes in his cupped palm. After a moment, he pulled his hand back through the window.

"Still snowing like hell out there, huh?"

It was an observation, not a question and a rather stupid statement, she thought, wondering if he was being sarcastic, rhetorical, or both. She looked around at the endless whiteness; the deep unbroken swells of snow stretching as far as she could see.

"I suppose so," she answered softly. "If Hell has winter."

There was an uncomfortable pause, then he answered flatly. "No, I really don't think that's the case."

She waited for more, but silence prevailed. Only the muffled idle of the car, the soft rhythmic puffing of exhaust from the tail pipe and the gentle plop of fat flakes on her damp head lent any substance to the moment.

As she stood beside the half-opened driver's window, she began to feel the cold work its icy fingers under her skin. For whatever reason, where before she could not—or would not—sense the intensity of the frigid air or the cutting wind; she now felt herself succumbing to the arctic elements. It seemed as if the longer she remained unsheltered in this environment the weaker her resistance became. Whatever magical spell had kept her oblivious to the freezing weather had all but left her. Her flesh pimpled under the thin polypropylene fabric of her workout gear, her stocking toes became anesthetized from the freezing wetness.

God. It's frigging cold!

In the next instant, as if the passing thought became material suggestion, she was shivering and her teeth began to chatter. If the man inside the car noticed her sudden discomfort, he said nothing. She puzzled for a moment, mildly concerned that she wasn't nearly as fearful as she intuitively assumed she should be.

"Would it be too much to ask if you could allow me to warm up a little?" she ventured. She rocked from side to side, shifting her weight from one numb foot to the other.

There was no response. She leaned farther forward, rising up on her toes again to peer through the small opening of the SUV's window. She folded her hands together and wedged them between her legs, seeking warmth from her groin.

The man remained silent, cloaked in shadow.

"I'm sorry to bother you, really," she managed through vibrating teeth. Her lips quivered from the cold. "But it's suddenly very cold out here. Very." She took a shaky breath, the icy air briefly paralyzing her lungs. When she next spoke, she was afraid that her jaw would not stop seizing long enough to articulate the words.

"Just a few minutes, and then I'll be on my way." She was pleading now and had no shame.

She might die in this wintry hell. Her breath clouded about her head in frantic uneven plumes.

"Where would you go?" he asked. The sound of his voice was both instantly reassuring and frightening. She actually pondered the question for what seemed a long while before stammering her response.

"I dunno." Her lips were completely numb and the words simply fell out of her mouth as a frosty sigh, breathed rather than spoken. Her eyes watered against a gust of glacial wind and she fought the urge to blink out of fear that her eyelids may freeze shut. Her lips struggled to form the word "please", but failed midway in the attempt.

There was a mechanical double-click as the doors of the Ford Expedition unlocked from within and the driver's side door swung open.

She leaned against the edge of the door, gazing into the dark interior of the car as a mirage of warmth ballooned forth and danced in the air. Her heart hammered in her chest and her stomach tightened with anticipation and relief.

She fell into the driver's seat as he slid over to make room.

~ * ~

After what seemed an uncomfortably long time, she mumbled a shy and cautious "Thank you". The heat from the vents blasted and the few stray strands of hair that had fallen out of her loose ponytail danced in the warm, dry currents.

She could feel his eyes on her—not in a lecherous sort of way—but rather curious and sadly protective, almost brotherly. She flushed with a sudden and surprising wash of shame and embarrassment. Rubbing the tops of her thighs vigorously, she hoped to bring warmth and circulation back to the frozen limbs.

"So," he finally asked. "Where was it you were thinking of going?" His voice was mellow and soothing without any trace of malice. "In stocking feet," he added with a slanted smile.

She stopped rubbing and repositioned herself in the driver's seat, stretching her long legs as far as she could within the shallow floor well of the driver's side. One of her soaked stocking feet caught on the corner of the gas pedal and the Expedition's engine roared in response. She jumped at the sound and struggled to free the snagged sock.

The engine revved a few more times while she tried to twist her foot free, then settled back into a quiet idle once she finally reached down and clumsily pulled the sock off her foot.

She slowly withdrew her hand from beneath the dash and dropped the matted grey sock in her lap. Her lower lip quivered from embarrassment as she turned to him and offered a shy and hesitant smile.

They made eye contact for the first time and her immediate reaction was both of surprise and recognition. She knew his face, yet strangely could not place him.

Thrones.

Devices.

The Crease.

The words, flavored with a tang of recollection and relevance, echoed weakly in her memory like a reflection of a distant melody or rhyme.

He returned the smile, soft and genuine, and then reached for the balled-up sock in her lap. She tensed, instantly protective of her personal space, yet did not stay his hand. Her stomach knotted then relaxed, her breath hitched and her mouth went dry.

He plucked the sock with two fingers and then wrung out the moisture in the space between his knees; water splashed hollowly against the floor mat in the passenger foot well. He then pulled the sock inside out and flattened it across the top of the dash just above the air vents.

He turned back to her and held out his hand, wiggling his fingers expectantly. The smile never left his eyes and his face remained warm and serene. She blinked, understanding his intent and reached down to remove the other sock. Eyes hooded with embarrassment, she quietly handed the soggy article over. He accepted, twisted the water from it and laid it to dry next to its mate.

"Thank you," she managed.

He shrugged and sat back in his seat.

She raised her feet out of the puddle of snowmelt and wiggled her toes in the jet of warm air blasting from the under the dash. They began to itch as they warmed.

In time—minutes or hours, she was unsure—she again broke the strangely comfortable silence.

"I'd ask you your name," she began with a shake of her head. "But I can't seem to remember my own." She chuckled nervously.

"Names aren't important here," he answered. "After all, it's not so much about who you were then; but rather, who and what you are now."

She glanced at him and chewed her lip as she puzzled over his cryptic response. Though strange sounding at first, what he said seemed... *right.*

He only smiled, and then sighed. "I can help you with both, actually." He reached forward, fingered open the glove box and pulled out something small enough to conceal in the palm of his hand.

She held her breath and watched his hands intently, bracing for a surprise.

"That's why I'm here," he explained with a smile. "Let me show you something."

He opened his hand, revealing a small digital phone resting face-up on his palm. He spun the phone around and flipped the face toward her. She leaned forward and stared at the glowing mini LCD screen.

Grainy photos cycled through a short slideshow of six digital stills, each image blinked on and then gave way to the next. First a man, then a woman, then the man again.

The man was terrifying to look at, with one dead eye and a menacing scar running the length of his right cheek. It seemed strange, almost contradictory, but in a calm and reassuring way she knew from the moment she saw him that she was meant to fear him.

The image of the woman, on the other hand, elicited a kind of terror that was normally reserved for the most lucid nightmares. The woman was beyond all reasonable doubt and against all rationale, unmistakable—undeniably—herself.

She again held her breath as the slideshow shifted through the six images; three foggy pictures of the threatening stranger with the blind eye alternating with unfamiliar pictures of herself.

He gently laid his hand over hers, startling her. Her eyes jumped to meet his deep gaze and as he spoke, she found herself immersed in his calmness.

"You recognized the woman, yes?"

Though the question would normally seem rhetorical, she knew that he wanted to be sure she not only could see that the images were of her; but that she also *accepted* it.

She nodded. Her eyes were wide, urgent and pleading.

He nodded once then continued, "And if you look deep into your memory, you will find that you remember me as well." He blinked and then cocked his head slightly.

Find a way into the Crease.

Eric McBride. The homeless John Doe. Asperger's savant.

Her Device.

It struck her as instantly as lightning seeking ground. He squeezed her hand and waited until she again met his gaze. When he spoke, his voice was no longer wholly his own, but rather all the voices of a lifetime's memories of voices. Both familiar and alien.

::Now, my Tyro, we haven't much time.::

Fifteen

"We haven't much time".

The voices came through in waves, disembodied and ephemeral. As she rose into consciousness, she perceived the conversation swinging in the air above her, alternating volleys of partial sentences that bounced to a fro as the speakers passionately argued their position.

"ICP... watch the shift... possible bleed... not certain from the CT... can't hurt to try... burr holes... Cushing's Triad."

The medical jargon didn't faze her; she knew they were discussing a patient with an obvious closed head injury resulting in elevated intracranial pressure. This was a rapidly progressive condition that, if not corrected through immediate decompression of the cranial cavity by drilling burr holes through the skull, could lead to severe brain damage or death.

She also knew on some intuitive level that she was, indeed, that particular patient. This did not bother her as much as she thought it might. In fact, it was a bit of a relief to be back in a place and time where *place* and *time* actually mattered. That snowy limbo between real and unreal had been a bit *too* real.

Alex lay perfectly paralyzed in a cognitive coma, unable to open her eyes yet becoming more aware of her surroundings as she emerged from the Crease.

Wow. She thought calmly. *That was easy.* That word and the shady, complex concept that enveloped it simply fell out of the darkness and seated itself in her consciousness.

The Crease.

The time she had spent there, the things she had been told and the images she'd been shown had only sharpened her perceptions of this world, preparing her for what she knew she must be ready to do when the time came. She had complete recall of her past travels and though she had been told that time was against them, she felt no pressure to achieve her mission. It was obvious that her physical body must be repaired before she could continue. There would have to be time enough for that.

She felt no pain as she lay there, yet she could sense the sudden warmth of a recently injected narcotic course through her veins.

"...morphine preop... to the OR in thirty... back here for recovery." The voices grew distant as the cottony blanket of pre-operative sedation settled down around her.

Obviously, she was going to surgery for emergency cranial decompression. So she must've survived the attack.

At least, so far.

If she was in her own hospital, as she assumed she must be, then she knew that she was in good hands—the neurosurgeon was skilled and efficient; the ICU staff, excellent.

What truly amazed her though, more than surviving a crushing blow to the head, was her complete and calm acceptance of all that had transpired. Each event, from before the assault to the surreal journey through the Crease to the ICU bed in which she now lay, remained crystal clear within her memory. What was before a jumbled unrelated mess was now a complete and vivid mosaic of causal events, key players and purposeful action.

The bizarre behavior of the two mysterious patients from her final night in Chicago, the cryptic writings of Eric McBride, the attack by the scarred Cyclops of a man and her experiences in the Crease were all interconnected in a tight and seamless weave of realities.

The world in which she grew up was merely a thin veneer laid clumsily over the world as it really was; and until her recent venture to the undefined edge, she had only known the smooth undisturbed center of that plateau.

But she had seen the outer reaches, had been to the frontier and into the fringe.

The Crease.

And now, she was back; armed with the knowledge and the power to take definitive action. Her enemies were many, she knew; but her target on this particular trip was singular, yet pivotal.

She felt her bed moving forward, the foot-end shimmied from a single wobbly wheel. From behind closed eyelids she sensed the bright fluorescents in the ceiling flare then fade as she passed under each. The OR team pushed her steadily down the long corridor that, in her sedated state, she vaguely remembered as the main hallway to the OR.

She thought about the man then, allowing his image to seep into her mind from the remembered photos and the crisp, total awareness that had evolved from her journey to and back from the Crease.

His scarred face and poisoned eye were forever etched into her memory, as was the sound of the oar slicing through the air. The image of the little girl's abandoned Razor scooter, her short pigtails flopping under the red hoodie and her still body recumbent in the belly of the kayak flashed through her mind with all the lucidity of lightning and the relentlessness of time.

Though he, as an individual, may or may not have been at all responsible for Cora's disappearance; she now knew that he indeed held communion with a family of malignant souls that were equally tempered by the seething fires of evil. And as such, he became a necessary target.

And though the vengeance she sought was not specifically hers to enjoy; she believed, nevertheless, that she would take some degree of lower-order pleasure in pushing him from the relative safety afforded by the center of this world to its shadowy and ill-defined edges...

...and into the crease of the next.

Sixteen

Gather the Witnesses—Legions of Thrones

Alex stepped cautiously from the shower and into a thick, absorbent robe. Her gait and balance improved daily, yet the smooth white tiles glistening with wetness beneath her bare feet still gave her pause. A rational post-surgical fear of relapse due to factors beyond her control was expected; however, just as pervasive was the secondary and potently superstitious terror of foolishly tripping over something as innocuous as a mislaid shoe or carelessly discarded pair of panties and thus whacking her already tender melon on the sharp corner of the porcelain vanity. Subsequently, she had removed all of the throw rugs in the house, and was now once again having that same internal argument over the wisdom of having laid a towel down to absorb her dangerously slick shower drippings versus the very real threat of that same towel becoming a fatal trip hazard.

With a certain healthy degree of morbid humor, she marveled at her newfound ability to occupy herself with such inane cautionary treatises. But then again, what else could she do. The hospital, though supportive throughout her recovery, was still reluctant to allow her back into the clinical fold and to care for patients.

She had only herself and time to kill.

That was a dark joke from some late-night black and white movie she got sucked into watching on AMC; and so she allowed herself another carefully allocated amount of graveyard humor to squelch the edginess.

That was how she referred to the creeping shadow of depression: edginess. She was beyond bored, yet secretly frightened—truly terrified—to step back into the awesome responsibilities of her anesthesia practice.

Granted, she had been given a full six weeks to recuperate and was five-sixths of the way there, but she still suffered from mild headaches—common from severe concussive injuries— and occasional double vision. They would want to reevaluate her extensively, testing both her cognitive and clinical skill sets. Alex remained confident in her abilities, though at times, in the wake of a throbbing headache or a bout of diplopia, she began to seriously doubt her future as an anesthetist.

Then, of course, there were the visions.

The reality, as hard to admit as it was and despite her reluctant optimism, was that the blow to her head and the subsequent surgery to relieve the pressure may have rendered her more of a liability than asset.

Her head...

She ran a hand over the shiny moist dome of her smoothly shaven scalp. Even though the neurosurgical prep team did a stellar job at shaving only the areas required for burr holes, and even cultivated some creative concealing layers from her previously thick locks; she opted for the Sinead O'Connor look anyway, out of both simplicity and adolescent defiance.

Looking now at her bald image in the foggy mirror, she actually felt that she more closely resembled Sigourney Weaver from one of the *Alien* movies in which the actress sported the same streamlined appearance. In her humble opinion, the alien-bashing Ripley was a much tougher broad than any has-been Irish pop star, and consequently more appealing. Either way, the look was hardly revolutionary and after over five weeks, she had to admit that it was starting to grow on her.

Grow on her. Get it?

She forgave herself that unintentional pun only because she refused to mourn her waist-length hair any longer. Besides, some unfortunate cancer victim was going to be on cloud nine when they got a hold of a brand new lid constructed from Alex's shorn mane through Locks of Love.

She sighed and rubbed a palm-full of eucalyptus infused lotion on her head. The camphor tingle was still fresh enough to surprise and delight. Her surgical scars, three semi-lunar crescents no larger than a half-dollar each, were knobby under her fingers. The healing pink skin was still insensate, numb to both touch and pinch as she tested it each morning and evening.

Also numb was the upper portion of the left half of her face, where an unnaturally straight, three-inch line of scar tissue ran horizontally across her cheek. She traced the still healing keloid with a gentle finger, feeling the indentation of her reconstructed facial bones and the concavity of the lower rim of her ocular orbit.

The flesh of her cheek, lower and upper eyelids, temple and portions of her brow remained completely numb from damage to the facial nerve. She tested a smile and then a frown, watching the asymmetry of her face as the muscles on that side remained flaccid, failing to contract without the appropriate neuronal intervention.

She clenched her teeth and breathed deeply for a single angry minute, recollecting the moment of the strike. She again felt the air cleaved by the blade of the kayak paddle an instant before the tapered edge dug into the side of her face and shattered the fragile bones, branding her forever.

It was a miracle that she had retained vision in that eye. Which made her think of *his* eye...

That eye. That fucked-up, rotten milk-colored, smoky-grey blind orb. In her dreams, it throbbed like a dead oyster in a cadaverous socket, mucoid and purulent.

Where was he right now?

A tickle of fear, then excitement ran through her body as she considered her assailant for the first time in a few weeks. But before the invigorating hum of acrimony could take hold, a calming warmth engulfed her as she allowed his image to resurface. She wanted to bask in anger and entertain vengeful thoughts, but a strange internal warmth quenched that desire, washing away all emotions but one.

Acceptance. Not forgiveness, empathy or even compassion. But simple, logical acceptance.

The empiricism of the emotion surprised her, and despite her efforts to bring back the stormy rage, she fell helplessly into the comfortable embrace of stone cold acceptance. Contrary to her initial assessment, the control of her savage emotion came not from within her but rather from a part of her that seemed tethered to something distant, far more grand and complex than either her ego or id.

As she gazed back at her reflection in the smeared fogginess of the mirror, she noticed a remarkable and inexplicable change in the appearance of her scars. The ragged and narrow trough of the facial scar dimpled slightly, then seemed to swell along the length as if trying to fill in by granulation. It didn't hurt. In fact, there was no sensation at all. Only the appearance of the linear scar actively healing under what she could only describe as time-lapse photography.

Her three scalp scars, too, seemed to be undergoing some sort of sudden and dramatic metamorphosis; swelling and gently pulsing, then gradually fading.

She ran a shaky hand over her scalp. The skin was smooth and unbroken, only slight ridges remained where the arcs of the scalp scars were shrinking. In minutes, proof of their presence at all was only evidenced by a faintly discolored pink shadow at each site.

The facial scar had faded as well, now only a dull lavender smear across her left cheek. Alex blinked, leaning closer into the mirror to reassess the phenomenon. Her wide-eyes darted from the top of her head to her cheek and back to the reflection of her own surprised gaze.

Before the shock of the surprising transformation could fully register, a single fat snowflake lit upon her shoulder. She considered the impossible frosty crystal, watching in the mirror as it melted against the skin of her naked shoulder. Another flake brushed against her upturned nose and yet the only thought that came to her mind was casual wonderment at the extreme odds of such a climatic phenomenon occurring within her bathroom.

She instinctively looked to the ceiling while thinking two simultaneous and contradictory thoughts: A snowstorm in her bathroom was insane. Impossible. Yet, under these circumstances, inspecting the textured ceiling above for evidence of a breech—a hole or tear in the roof—seemed like the rational, logical thing to do.

A calming sense of rightness swelled around her, enveloped her completely; and after seeing for herself that her bathroom ceiling remained intact, she looked again to her reflection in the mirror. Her scars had completely disappeared, as had her baldness.

In the mirror, her hazy reflection wore long raven hair dusted white from the increasing snowfall. Fluffy pregnant flakes gently encrusted the crown of her head; some tumbled under their own inscrutable weight as gossamer folds of snow-lace cascaded over her shoulders.

She chanced a glimpse away from the mirror and took in the reality of her surroundings. Her bathroom remained steamy, the air humid and without snowfall. She ran her hand over the flesh of her head and again felt the fresh ridges of the burr hole ports. She rubbed her left cheek; her fingertip following the shallow groove of the oar's imprint, tracing the defect.

She looked again into the fantasy world within the mirror and her fresh, unblemished face gazed back, framed by lush ribbons of velvety sable hair, flecked with large snowflakes. The *before* version of Alex?

Another vision.

A small voice, perhaps the decaying remnant of a sleepy and fleetingly transcendent Earth-bound consciousness, told her that this was one hell of a hallucination. But she found it far too easy to dismiss that explanation, despite its inherent logic. So instead, she willfully conceded to the beautiful and irrational calling that spoke in the language of the Crease.

The voice whispered.

More oracle than muse, the foreign—yet equally familiar—resonance filled her with hope and knowledge. She immediately recognized the thrill of flexing ancient mental muscles that had learned to simply shed atrophied logic like dead skin cells.

A smile touched the corners of her mouth as she recognized the vibration of her Device and the welcome chill of the Crease as it called her back.

In the background of her reflected image, the bathroom structures faded away as the snowfall thickened to an iridescent cataract. White tiled walls, cream colored towels on racks, and frosted shower glass all began to shift into translucency, their substance thinning until Alex began to fall forward, both physically and consciously, toward the universe within the mirror and closer to the frozen emptiness of space and time redefined.

The voice, as comfortable as the elusive memories of the womb, sang melodiously through her head and she smiled deeply. The tightness of the emotion spread pleasantly through the cells of her being, and even as the echoes of the single not-quite-spoken phrase reverberated through her head, she vividly recalled her mission.

::It is nearly time.::

Spoken evenly, the masculine voice from the swirling dark eternal winter of the Crease carried the authority of ageless knowledge.

How soon?

::Very near.:: The answer was more thought than spoken word, less language than unrefined energy.

::Strengthen yourself,:: It directed. *::And learn.::*

And with a near audible snap and a lightning quick blink, she was back in her bathroom standing before the frosted mirror.

A smiling bald woman stared back at her as the thinning tendrils of shower steam coiled around her glistening head. Though she felt the lingering smile tugging at her lips, she could see that the face reflected in the mirror was slightly crooked on one side. A single straight scar stretched across the top of her left cheek, deforming the usual creases that would normally accentuate her natural smile.

"Gather the witnesses," she whispered.

"Legions of Thrones."

Seventeen

A prototypical Michigan winter drifted across the middle of the state in a series of frosty snow showers, accumulations layering on top of one another from early November through the crescendo of the holiday shopping season, until by Christmas the river valley was dressed in nearly sixteen inches of crusty ice and snow.

Alex split her free time, which was essentially all of her time, between arduous physical workouts in her basement on the used Soloflex, and sifting through the volumes of data from her Internet researches on religion and mythology. Most days it remained cold enough for her to keep a constant fire burning in the moderate hearth, yet today the fireplace smoldered weakly in the wake of an unexpected warming spell. Across the hazy white acreage behind her ranch-style home, patches of muddy green were bleeding through the irregular mounds of melting snow. The thick fog that had slid over the surface of the river throughout the warming afternoon now crawled up the sloped backyard toward the rear of the house.

Despite the climbing temperature outside, a persistent moist chill stiffened her blood and needled her joints. The left side of her face ached horribly. Earlier, she had lit and kept a fire, but now as the embers smoldered she watched the rolling fogbank boil over the banks of the swollen river, the waters pregnant with snow melt and the air supersaturated with vapor. Sitting in a modest well-used recliner in front of the dying fire, she stared out the expansive windows of the walkout basement and watched winter temporarily die.

It was still early January, so the aberrant thaw was only a tease and actually more of an inconvenience as the forecast for the coming week called for below freezing temperatures to return. The slush and soft ice would rapidly refreeze, becoming more treacherous as the climate rallied back to the frigid.

She sipped from a wide steaming mug of coffee and watched six deer—all doe—forage in the sloppy wooded yard.

Over five months had passed since her surgery and she hadn't been outside of the house once. Not that she couldn't or even wouldn't, but she simply didn't feel it was necessary.

That's what was important to her now, things that were *necessary*.

All that she needed—food, sundries, cleaning supplies, even the firewood—could be and, indeed, were delivered. She was now focused on more necessary things...

Like her research.

And the surprise that had awaited her this afternoon at her front door.

~ * ~

The doorbell had chimed twice before she could reach the front door on the upper level of the house from her basement office. She bounded up the flight of carpeted stairs—taking them two at time, while pulling on her thick fleece cardigan—as the echoes of Westminster Chimes reverberated off the vaulted ceilings.

As she emerged from behind the basement door and turned toward the foyer, she could see clearly through the sidelights framing the wide mahogany front door that a bulky shadow rocked back a forth just outside the entry. The dark swaying movement paused for a moment as an extension of the shadowy figure reached toward the door. The bell tolled again, the musical notes louder on this level of the house.

"Coming", she sang out. "Just a sec."

She reached for, grasped—and before some remote psychic whisper could finish its warning—turned and pulled the thick brass knob. The thumb lock disengaged with a tactile click, solid and forcefully vivid. It reminded her of the snapping sound a car door's locks made when popping open all at once. It was a familiar mechanical click that signaled a great change in both her security and her perception of risk.

Surprising herself, she swung the door open at the same time the prudent voice in her head screamed for her to stop.

Deadbolt the door and run. Load the pistol stashed under the bed.

Instead of heeding the distant internal warning, she found herself staring at the middle of a man's wide back. He stood beneath the arched overhang, tall and clad in thick winter gear. At the sound of the door scraping the warped oak threshold, he slowly turned to face her.

She froze; and for the longest second in her life she was certain that her heart had stopped completely. The air in her lungs condensed into an icy vacuum.

His head was tilted down, looking at the paperwork tacked to his narrow clipboard; but even shaded by the shallow brim of his fur winter cap she could make out his face.

And the patch over his right eye.

When her paralysis finally broke, her hand flew to her face, caressing the scar along her cheek. She held her fingers gently over that portion of her face, attempting to conceal the mark as if by preventing him from seeing it she may also prevent him from recognizing her and then go about finishing that which he started five months earlier on the bank of the bubbling river.

Her gaze quickly dropped to his hands fully expecting to see the splintered oar nestled in his firm grasp, knuckles white as he flexed his grip in preparation to let it fly, the bloody edge of the paddle blade slicing through the air with a sinister whistle.

But his thick gloved hands held only the clipboard. Misaligned pages clamped under the metal fastener fluttered in the mild breeze.

He gazed at her curiously for but a second, his one eye flitting across her features, trying to pry behind her splayed fingers for a glimpse of the mottled and bumpy flesh beneath. His lips drew tight, as if to speak and then relaxed as he nodded, glanced back down at his paperwork and then flipped over the cover sheet on his clipboard.

When he dipped his head again, she finally noticed the U.S. Postal Service patch sewn into the fur of his dark blue pile cap. His thick Gortex parka and snow pants were also the uniform blue of a United States Postal carrier.

She finally allowed her lungs to contract and then expand again in a shuddery cycle. Her breath plumed in thin smoky ribbons.

"Afternoon, ma'am." His voice was deep and sad. "Unusually warm today."

She stared at the top of his head with an anxious mixture of shock, anger and dread until he looked back up and locked on her eyes. His one cold orb stared, unblinking and steely blue-gray.

"Ma'am?"

She felt weak and energized at the same time, the part of her standing in this world wanted to slam the door in his stony face and run; while the transformed part of her—that ancient self—wanted to lash out and claw the remaining eye from his narrow skull.

"Ma'am?"

She blinked then and resisted the urge to shake her head in a desperate attempt to clear the damnation from her vision.

He gently pushed a bulky manila envelope toward her, the paper and packaging tape crinkled under the grasp of his gloved hand.

She glanced at the proffered package, barely recognizing her familiar name and address neatly printed across the front in block letters, while completely spacing on the return information in the sender's corner. She accepted it with both hands, more out of habit than willingness; handling the delivery as if it might begin to squirm out her grasp, slither down the steps and into the surrounding woods.

"I'll need a signature." He had rotated the clipboard around and tipped it toward her with one gloved hand, while offering a scratched silver pen with the other—now ungloved and raw from exposure.

It seemed as if the air between their hands grew thick and hot as her fingers moved to grab the pen. The motion was involuntary, but natural, and as the distance closed, the ancient incarnation of Alex screamed from unsounded depths in defiance. She was certain that if their fingers touched—if she inadvertently brushed against his cold flesh—she would crack and wail like a banshee.

The distance closed, the pen wavered slightly in his loose grip. Her fingers stretched and trembled.

And then the pen was in her hand; she scratched something across the wrinkled page, dropped the pen onto the clipboard, and quickly pulled her hand to her breast. He deftly spun the clipboard, flipped the pen into the air, caught it at the top of its arc and tucked it neatly into a small slit in one of the folds of his parka. He winked and nodded once.

"Thank you," he said flatly. Alex felt a dome of nausea rise from the coil of her bowels. She consciously fought the urge to puke and run.

He paused for a moment, cocked his head slightly as if to ask a question, then pouted his pale narrow lips. In that brief moment, goose flesh rose as something akin to fever chills crawled up her spine. If he were to recognize her and suddenly strike, it would be in that frozen frame of time. She was also certain that, hopelessly paralyzed with fear and without a fight, she would die silently on her own doorstep.

Instead, he turned on his heels and stepped off the porch in a splash of dirty slush.

"Have a safe afternoon," he offered as he strode toward his dirty white mail-truck.

Not 'have a *good* afternoon', but 'have a *safe* afternoon'.

She remained in the doorway, dead still, watching him pull down the circle drive and onto the street. As the small mail truck turned out of the drive, she saw his face reflected in the stretched rectangular rearview mirror mounted on the right side of the vehicle. His features vibrated sharply in the reflection from the bounce and quake of the truck, but she could clearly see his one steel grey eye staring coolly, intently back at her.

~ * ~

Alex sipped from her thick coffee mug, the dark brew now tepid and gone bitter. She rocked gently in the recliner and watched the last of the caramel-colored deer scrounge along her rolling back yard for bits of tasty morsels that had become exposed during the surprise thaw.

Her heart, still swollen with fear, seemed to skip an occasional beat; yet the rate and rhythm had slowed considerably. She could still taste the coppery tang of adrenaline and bitterness of bile along the back of her tongue, an acrid palate that even the dark roast of coffee could not expunge. The trepidation and paranoia of victimization kept her more edgy and alert than any strength of caffeine, and she was mildly amused, if not supremely astonished, at the calm certainty with which she awaited his inevitable return.

She could visualize his clunky form crashing through the glass of the basement doors: face slashed to bloody ribbons from the shards, the torn eye patch dangling from one tattered strap, strong arms brandishing the splintery wooden oar.

She waited with a commitment to finality.

So when dusk pulled a hazy blanket over the day, and the fog grew thick with fat droplets of clinging moisture, and he failed to burst through the sliding glass doors, she sighed with a faint measure of relief and closed her eyes against the night.

Exhausted from the fearful wait, sleep threatened but failed to take hold. Instead, she shifted in her seat and crossed her legs beneath her. The fire was nothing but powdery ash and the hearth provided no warmth.

She glanced at the unopened package lying on the side table next to her chair and again recalled the malignant mailman's visit from earlier in the day. With a sinking sense of dread, she suddenly realized that before today, all of her mail and packages had been left inside the mudroom door.

She never had to sign for anything. That was the agreement she had made with the post office. She just forgot, answered the door out of habit...

She marveled she hadn't made the connection before today, but then soon reconciled the fact she had never actually met her mailman before the attack...

Or since.

Most people, during the course of their lives—if they live in the same house long enough—will eventually have the opportunity to come face to face with their mail carrier. Whether while mowing the lawn, shoveling snow, or taking the trash to the curb, somewhere down the line a person generally winds up accepting their mail from the postman or woman directly, often with a smile and some inane small talk about the weather or the local sports teams.

Unless, of course, you chose not to go out.

The fact that her mailman was the same cretin that tried to remove her head with an oar was too surreal to chalk up to mere coincidence.

A dark hood of depression descended over her—pressing—but before it could establish any significant foothold, a welcome tingle caressed the base of her skull.

The Push.

With some effort, she could now summon that ability, harnessing the telepathic connection nearly at will. But sometimes it still came unannounced and with an intent all its own.

With a hesitant finger, she spun the bulky package so that she could read the addresses beneath the sheen of the wrinkled cellophane label. Her name and address were hand-printed in large neat block letters across the middle while the name of a large, well-known pharmaceutical supplier adorned the upper left corner.

While moving to Michigan and then eventually taking the job at the hospital had fulfilled the need to start her life anew; the salary was modest and the workload light. Therefore, she began supplementing both her income and her desire for autonomous practice by moonlighting at various office based surgi-centers. She had worked out a deal with the administrators of these smaller independent operations that if they could provide her with the necessary equipment to perform the required anesthetics, then she would assume responsibility for procuring the medications essential to her craft.

After the Incident, as her insurance company referred to the attempt on her life, her office-based assignments defaulted to other providers in the surrounding area. Though she lost a great deal of revenue from the lack of work and possibly even more credibility in that market, her accounts with the pharmaceutical supplier had remained active. She never thought to cancel her usual standing supply order; nor had she ever given the previous two deliveries a moment's thought, placing the similar packages where she always had before the Incident—atop the dryer in the laundry room where she would remember to scoop them up on her way to one of the three sites.

Now with this third package, cool and dry in her hands, she reflected on the contents: small vials of creativity. But did she have the courage to take the next necessary step?

To bring things to an end? To finally know peace?

The electric tickle from the Crease pulsed with reassurance and enlightenment, ebbing with an energetic tide of its own unique design. Reaching across time, it validated her confidence by gently pressing her thoughts in the right direction.

The *necessary* direction.

The wave of Push hummed with approval and her senses vibrated with comprehension. She sighed as the lucidity of the moment sharpened her perceptions of both responsibility and irony.

She began working at the glued seam of the sealed envelope with a short fingernail.

Eighteen

Alex awoke facedown in the powdery snow of the Crease.

The chill of the melting fluff on her lips enlivened her, the furry weight of the crisp flakes on her eyelashes tickled. Within seconds she was fully alert and pushing herself from prone to squatting.

Keeping a low profile and resting her elbows on her upturned knees she quickly scanned the smooth white horizon for any sign of the man she had brought with her. Her vision was aided by the milky iridescence mysteriously emanating from the surrounding snow.

There was no active snowfall this trip back; only the thin skeins of snow dust—as fine as talc—that cascaded off her as she stood to her full height. The night air was sedate, with little to no wind; the only sound seemed to whisper from between her pursed lips as she exhaled. Even her breath, slightly staccato from the tension, plumed around her in an unmolested cloud of vapor to hang in the air, a frosted billowy web suspended in the still winter night.

As she turned one full circle, she narrowed her eyes and searched strenuously into the blinding abyss of the arctic-like void. The snowscape stretched as far as she could see, a rolling white blanket of unbroken softness that ultimately interfaced with the deep blackness of the vaulted night sky forming the unbroken rim of the horizon.

Her feet shuffled in the snow as she turned, crunching hollowly with each half step. Frozen clumps of snow flopped over the tops of her tennis shoes and saturated her socks with melt. She brought her hands to her face to both wipe the moisture from her cheeks and to shield her vision from the eerie phosphorescent glare of blinding eternity.

She sniffled softly as a small drop of snowmelt crept to the tip of her nose; blinking her eyes and refocusing as she continued to scan the distance. She eventually took a deep breath and held it, hoping it might amount to a cleansing and clarifying sigh, when she finally saw him.

The air trapped in her lungs instantly froze, shrank, and then in another instant expanded so rapidly she blew the entire volume through clenched teeth in a screeching whistle.

There he was, made small and vulnerable by the distance: a vague fleshy outline against the stark continuity of the endless white sprawl. Sitting in the otherwise smooth snow, he appeared as a malignant pale bump against the sweeping white frontier. His legs were splayed out in front of him and his head drooped against his chest. His arms hung limply at his sides and his rounded back heaved spasmodically.

It appeared as though he was sobbing and the instant that observation registered with her, a wave of nausea washed over her. The thought of this animal possessing any emotion that would cause him to cry revolted her. Real sadness, not flaky melancholy, was a human emotion borne from pain and suffering—loss of love and hope—and a stifling tsunami of remorse; not self-pity or fear. Those were the few things about her ever-changing universe in which she was confident.

Having intimate experience with pain and loss as well as self-pity and remorse had made her a reluctant expert on that vast topic.

She watched for a moment longer as the naked man's figure hitched with the irregular hiccoughs of silent weeping. He pulled his legs weakly to his chest, hugged them tightly, and then let them fall defeatedly back into snow.

The effects of the paralytic that killed him had most likely worn off and what she observed now was not the signature muscle weakness of emergence from the drug, but rather a confused and vain attempt to come to terms with his new and bizarre surroundings. His last recollection was also Alex's to share, the wide-eyed shock and anger of being assaulted by a much smaller woman. And then the equally wide-eyed assent of dismay and terror as the needle pierced his skin.

Killing him had only been the first step of the process.

He had returned to Alex's house only three days after he finally realized who she was; this time, however, without mail or packages. Prodded by nagging suspicions and eventually recognizing her from the photo directory hanging in the hospital's main lobby, he carried instead a parcel of long, sharp serrations concealed within the bulk of his winter parka.

She had answered on the second chime of the bells, eased the door wide and silently invited him to cross the threshold. She looked exhausted, as if just awakened from an unplanned afternoon nap. Her face had been expressionless.

All too easy, he had thought. He fingering the ten-inch blade tucked beneath his arm as he stepped into the open entry...

Initially flattened by a pair of in-line rollerblades swung in a perfect arc by their knotted laces, he dropped to the marbled stone of the foyer like a sack of fetid laundry. Blood pulsed freely from where the toes of the skates laid opened his temple, covering his patched eye in a thick wash of crimson.

Acting quickly and confidently, Alex had straddled the man, pinioning his arms with both knees. Reaching for his jaw, her grip had slipped twice in the sluice of blood before she secured his face by the mandible and wrenched his head to the side so that his one good eye stared up at her. Both repulsed and energized by his glazed look, she leaned close and whispered fervently into his face.

"I am your end!"

With that, Alex had found the prominent external jugular vein among the taught cords of his neck, palpated it with her thumb, uncapped the hypo with her teeth and thrust the needle deep into the bulging vessel. Dark swirls of blood swam within the barrel of the syringe seconds before she depressed the plunger, sending twenty cc's of the potent paralytic coursing through his body.

He had recovered from the stun of the roller blades' inertia just in time to appreciate the debilitating muscular fasciculation of succinylcholine. As the drug saturated his tissues and completely polarized every neuromuscular junction in his body for the very last time, his single eye momentarily cleared through the growing weakness.

Alex then leaned back on her haunches and firmly held his gaze as the waves of paralysis turned the man's body into an inert sack of dying flesh. She quickly calculated the time it would take for a total myocardial infarction from global hypoxia and then leaned forward one last time and watched through the window of his solitary eye as he died.

At the exact moment that his physical body became a lifeless shell and his soul flailed about the cosmos for direction, she had seized his essence and brought him here.

Alex now clenched her hands into small fists at her sides, set her jaw tight, and strode through the deep snow toward the man. Each heavy step brought her close enough to the seated figure to recognize more details of his face. As his features clarified and her anger grew, the intensity of that rogue emotion was as equally tempered by a calming determination that swelled in sync with each new wave of raw vengeance.

She recognized the voice of the Crease and that it was feathering her rage, refining the energy and refocusing it as a psychic beam onto the target.

He might have heard her approach, now a mere twenty paces away, as she crunched through the frozen crust of snow; but more likely he sensed the warmth of Balance reaching for him, an unwelcome wave of heat that throbbed ahead of the advancing legion of Thrones.

He turned, a twitchy jerk of his head that brought him face to face with Alex. He was without his eye patch and she found herself staring into the dark hollow hole of an empty socket. Apparently that deformed eye had actually been a crude prosthetic made of some material that was unable to make the crossover into the universe of the Crease.

Like an instinctual awakening, Alex became more aware of this newly discovered ancient world with each excursion. She was now more Device than Tyro. Although the absolute timelessness of it terrified and confused her, she still felt *necessary* to the overall fabric of the Crease; as if she had always been a primary constituent of its grandeur and complexity.

As she watched his single bloodshot eye search her face frantically for answers, his thin lips quivered and his chalky skin dimpled with the goose flesh of terror rather than cold.

Anger, primitive and raw, contorted his face as he hissed at her. His hands, gnarled into weak claws, rolled in the thick snow at his sides like small rodents writhing in the silent throes of sudden death.

"You," he stammered. "You brought me here." The words trailed off into the silent frozen night. He shook his head in dismay.

"Imposs... ible," he whispered in a shaky stutter, looking down at his nakedness.

He again shook his head and then gazed up at her. The moisture that glazed his one eye reflected her own stony features, and as she recognized her face in that convex pool she refused to ascribe any quality of humanity to him by accepting the wetness as tears. His mouth spasmed as his lips worked desperately around a grill of crooked teeth, trembling like dying purple worms as they tried to find the most effective, if not appropriate words.

Confusion replaced fear, and then morphed back into anger as he glared at Alex.

"No," she stated softly. "It's not at all impossible."

She slowly squatted, dropping herself to his eye level. When she had his undivided, unblinking attention, she leaned very close, bringing her nose within millimeters of his, both of her eyes locked on to his one. The effort to focus her vision at such a close distance strained her ocular muscles, but the subtle throb behind her brow energized and honed her intensity as she began to reveal to him that which she now fully and coherently understood.

A sudden lucidity, unlike anything she ever experienced, washed through her, filled her soul to the brim and then flowed smoothly out of her in a flood of confident testament. An invisible shroud of lightness and warmth enveloped her, sentient and powerful, yet weightless. This transparent cloak seemed at first, foreign, but then became familiar—comforting and welcome. Ecstasy filled her, so pure and innocent that it could only have originated before the womb. She grew detached from herself and that which she thought she once understood, while at the same time her soul became completely infused with ancient knowledge.

She was not-Alex and wholly-Alex at the same instant, the flux between the two states occurring so fast that the boundaries blurred as the spiritual, virtual, and actual swirled together in a slurry of new reality.

She shifted, tilting her head to the side as she brushed against his dry cheek. The touch of his cold skin sent a tickle of revulsion through her stomach, but only the distant and shrinking human portion of Alex responded to that visceral stimulus.

"In fact," she whispered just shy of his ear. "It's quite necessary."

Alex now fully realized that she had been both bait and facilitator and was now being called upon as a historian.

"You have denied your gift and brought upon yourself a wrath worthy of eternity." Her voice faded as the winds of the Crease rolled from the edges of the horizon across the endless frozen snowfields toward their position. The newborn tempest blasted them and soundlessly spiraled around the epicenter of Alex and the man.

She was now the homing device, a targeting beam for the advancing swarm of Thrones: the avenging entities of the Crease where true judgment took place.

A new voice, genderless and without any quality of sound, reverberated in both of their minds. The gale-force thought slammed them both with silent, immeasurable decibels.

::The true work of man is the burden of love.:: It pronounced.

Unfazed by the psychic echoing and looking down upon the trembling naked man, Alex stood. She watched him intently, but he averted his gaze and sobbed dryly into his cyanotic hands.

The hurricane raged silently, spinning a column of blinding snow to surround them in a widening cylinder of whiteness that grew ever taller. Not a single flake of snow touched either of them inside of the protective sheath as the storm spun and kneaded the curved walls of the column higher into the black vault of the night.

Alex gazed up through the perfectly round opening that was the eye of the storm and watched as the countless stars began to turn across the canopy of darkness above. While the walls of the cylinder churned and swirled in counter-clockwise eddies and whorls, the stars on high spun in opposition—clockwise—against the current of the storm in a rapidly accelerating vortex. Stars of all size and age left their orbits and contributed their mass to the growing density of the evolving galaxy above. As more cosmic material was added to the spiraling vortex, potential gravity became actual and sheer mass began to pull the matter down into the circular volume of the churning cylinder, extending a brilliant funnel into the maw.

Alex smiled and looked back down at the man, whom must have felt the great weight of the universe bearing down on him because he now stared in terrified awe at the top of the cylinder. He cringed from the sight of the blazing white vortex as the probing finger pressed into this world, a cosmic tornado of star-stuff and collapsed time seeking to touch down and devour that which had become unnecessary.

The man fell onto his back and curled his legs into his naked form, trying feebly to pull himself into a protective fetal ball. His mouth was frozen in a silent scream, his one eye paralyzed and fixed on the advancing spike of white energy, while the skin around his vacant eye-socket twitched involuntarily.

Tiny fragments of the blinding galactic twister flaked from the narrow funnel as it spun with ferocious velocity. The small flecks of energy separated from the vortex and floated gently down the shaft of the column, not unlike snow in a windless storm.

The quantity of the flakes grew as the spinning finger of eternity shed more and more mass. Soon the silent air of the cylinder was filled with a blizzard of gently falling fluff, dancing and seesawing on the light currents of calm downdrafts as the turbulent cosmic funnel spiraled feverishly above.

Alex turned her face up to the falling flakes and allowed them to accumulate on her cheeks, her closed eyelids, and her moist lips. When they lit upon her skin, the flakes melted to dry dusty talc then faded to nothing. When she opened her eyes, she noticed that the flake-fall thickened the air around her, yet not a single speck had accumulated on the snowy ground. Then she looked down at the man and saw something completely different.

Where the flakes landed on his flesh, small areas of excoriation erupted. The flakes instantaneously disintegrated, leaving in their passing grey lesions that soon reddened and then collapsed. Many of the wounds widened as they deepened, exposing the flesh by layers. The holes did not bleed, and as more flakes covered his naked form and began to dissolve the tissue, the digested areas expanded and meshed.

Alex watched coolly, without emotion, as witness to the event.

"*You* have become unnecessary," she proclaimed evenly.

His face no longer resembled anything that could be called a face, and he therefore made no sound as the universe consumed him.

Nineteen

"Could you direct us to the surgical department?"

The woman they had stopped and asked directions from wore light blue scrubs, bright purple rubber Crocs on her feet, and a waist-length floral cover-up that matched her bouffant head cap. She held a square Styrofoam food container in one hand as she gestured down the hall with the other.

"Yep, OR's right down there and through the double doors. You gotta get buzzed in, though." She raised her eyebrows and quickly scanned the fronts of their overcoats for nametags. "You guys reps?" she asked.

"No, we're actually here to speak with someone from anesthesia."

"C'mon, I'll badge you in." She turned to lead them down the corridor.

At the threshold she swept her name badge across a small square black box embedded in the wall next to the thick double doors. After a musical chime and a loud mechanical click, both doors swung smoothly inward. The woman led them a few steps into the wide white hallway beyond and motioned again with her free hand.

"Anesthesia office is the second door on the left, though I don't know if anyone's in there right now," she explained. "They might all be on cases at the moment."

The two men nodded and thanked her as she disappeared into a small lounge.

Doctors David Rose and Richard Linc walked softly down the hall toward the half-open door of the anesthesia office.

The outside of the thick oak door was adorned with three schedule calendars—this month, last month, and the next. Names were carefully printed in each square, while some were crossed out with red ink and scribbled over in blue. Various memos and a few Far Side cartoons completed the montage.

Richard Linc quickly perused the assignment calendars and noticed the conspicuous absence of one name. He made eye contact with David Rose; they both grimaced and then sighed. Rose reached for the thick metal handle just as the door swung open and a tall fat man in stained green scrubs nearly bowled them over.

"Whoa! Shit, partner. Didn't see you there. Sorry." The man dramatically regained his balance, clasping his hands to his barrel chest in mock surprise. Rich and David smiled weakly and nodded forgiveness.

"Can I help you fellas?"

"Yes, we're actually here to see one of your CRNAs," Rich answered. He struggled to keep his voice even and under control; yet when he uttered the name, his usual smooth baritone cracked.

"Alex D'Meiter."

The seconds that passed were torture for the two men as they watched the huge man before them work his pale jowls and knot his brow in frustration. For one frightening moment, Rich felt that they might have the wrong hospital and that he and David had driven up from Chicago for nothing.

The big man rubbed his fleshy cheeks with one round hand, pulling the pillowy skin around his eyes as he did.

"No, can't say that I know who that is," he finally responded. "'Course, I am on loan here. Only been here one week of a two month gig, so…"

"Excuse me." A voice startled them from behind. "Can I help you gentleman?" They both turned and met the stern gaze of a stout woman in blue scrubs. Her face was cut stone, framed by a closely cropped head of salt and pepper hair.

She extended her hand as she introduced herself. "Emily McBride, OR coordinator." Her eyes alone demanded the unspoken; and the two men, immediately recognizing the innate severity of a nurse manager from their own experiences in the OR, made the necessary introductions.

"Greg," she said to the fat man after shaking Rich and David's hands and nodding solemnly to each. "Can you give Rachael a break in three?"

The mountainous anesthetist shrugged as he squeezed through the doorway and past the group. "Sure, you bet."

When he had turned the corner, Emily took a deep breath and sighed heavily. She looked over each of the men and then gestured for them to follow her.

They crossed the hall and stepped into a similar office as the previous, yet without the clutter. She gently closed the door behind them and immediately took a seat at the small corner desk. There was only one other chair available, so both men elected to stand. Emily swiveled her chair to face the men as they stood somewhat nervously alongside two silver file cabinets. David placed his hands in his trench coat pockets and clenched his fists to keep from fidgeting. Rich leaned carefully against one of the cabinets for support.

"So, what really brings you here?" she finally asked.

David and Rich exchanged glances for a second, then Rich spoke, his voice regaining some the clarity that he had lost earlier.

"Well, as we explained earlier, we are friends of Alexandra D'Meiter. From Chicago." He paused and swallowed, looking quickly at David, who nodded in affirmation.

"And we were just hoping to see her," he finished.

Emily frowned, chewed the inside of her cheek and then huffed once as she shook her head.

"You're friends of hers and you drove all the way up from Chicago to see her without phoning first to see if she would even be available?"

David narrowed his eyes and shook his head in mild frustration, exasperated by the woman's interrogation. But before he could challenge, Rich shot right back at her.

"Why should it matter to you?" He asserted, firm yet calm. "We wanted to surprise her and—"

"It matters, Doctor, because Alex was a dear friend of mine and I simply don't recall her ever mentioning the two of you."

Her use of the past tense nearly escaped Rich, and as soon as he registered it she was back at them. "When was the last time either of you spoke to Alex?"

David had pulled his hands from his coat pockets, but his fists remained clenched. He opened his mouth to rebut, his face reddened with anger. Rich spoke before David could attack, and the anesthesiologist's voice was so deep and soft that David froze.

"Emily, what aren't you telling us?"

She narrowed her glare, eyeing Rich's face for any suspicious wrinkle, any hint of misrepresentation. Suddenly her granite features softened, the concrete veneer crumbled a bit and her eyes widened with realization.

"You really don't know, do you?" she breathed sadly.

"What?" David spat the words out sharply.

Emily's eyes darted from David to Rich, then settled on the blank cream-colored wall between them. She sighed, and this time the exhalation tapered into the quaver of a near sob.

"Alex," she began, her voice a mere whisper. "Died over eight months ago."

~ * ~

They sipped their coffee silently, each processing the unexpected news in a different and personal way. David Rose toyed with the empty sugar packets, folding and creasing them hard against the table—a surgeon always striving for order and control where there simply was none. In the wake of irrepressible time, the events that encompassed and defined Alexandra D'Meiter had passed without a moment's consideration for David or his hubris. Providence, it seemed, had a mathematical foundation all its own.

Richard Linc sat motionless, his long arms tucked neatly between his legs, his hands folded loosely. He seemed to stare placidly into empty space; but his mind agonized at the speed of memory, frantically sorting the emotional from the reasonable. The spatial disconnect between the cognitive present, the bittersweet past and the anonymous future created a psychic vertigo that was mildly nauseating. Outwardly, he remained stoic if not somewhat exhausted.

A muffled squeak of rubber on tile echoed in the nearly empty cafeteria. Richard broke his trance in time to see that Emily was walking toward their table. Her stride was ambling, almost burdened; yet she carried only a thin file folder under one arm while balancing a dark shoebox on the palm of the other. Her waist-length scrub coat was open and rustled around her thick hips as she approached. Watching the pastel fabric flow behind her in the silent breezes, he couldn't ignore an accidental vision.

For the briefest of moments—a flash, really—Richard likened the nurse to a humble middle-aged angel on a wingless advance to deliver some terrible or wonderful prophecy. Even the graying blond in her hair, caught in the fluorescent haze of the industrial ceiling panels, seemed ablaze with cold heavenly fire.

Although surprised by his spontaneous capacity for theological fancy, Richard quickly blinked away the spurious vision and religious allusions, and gave the nurse a tired, earthly smile.

She returned the greeting with her own wan expression and took a seat in the remaining chair. She placed the box softly on the flecked plastic surface of the table, startling David from his sugar-packet origami. He blinked erratically a few times and then ran a thick hand through his disheveled hair.

"The OR schedule just finished up," she stated as a matter of fact in an attempt to open conversation. Both men simply nodded.

She gently pushed the shoebox across the table toward David. His gaze followed, but he made no effort to accept it. Emily sighed heavily, and then with the conviction of a patient matriarch she said, "You must be Cora's father. She had your eyes."

David tensed, swallowed thickly and then chewed his lower lip. When he brought his gaze to meet hers, she held it coolly and confidently yet without scrutiny or prejudice.

"Despite her natural charm and easy spirit," she said, "Alex shared very little with those of us she allowed into her circle. I felt honored—no, blessed—to have been considered one of her closest friends.

"She told me about her daughter, and of course the father." She nodded at Dave. "She only spoke of the disappearance once and never in detail." Emily took a deep breath and held it for some time before continuing.

When she spoke next her voice dropped to a soft confessional whisper. "I'm ashamed to admit that I assumed the worst and simply figured that the father was to blame. I never pressed the issue. It was an obvious open wound on Alex's heart."

She stunned David next when she reached for his hand and gave a firm squeeze.

"You must know, David, that she never once spoke ill of you. Ever." She paused until he again met her eyes. She then smiled and squeezed his hand even harder. "I couldn't see it then from just the pictures; but of course, now..." She tilted her head slightly. The limelight of the overhead fluorescents caught the gentle curve of her eye and sparked a lustrous glint.

"You do have your daughter's eyes," she said softly. "There's no malice there."

They shared the silent moment looking at one another across the table, tacitly exchanging both approval and gratitude.

"Her things. Pictures and what-not." Emily finally gestured to the box. David eventually swept the cardboard container into his lap but did not open it.

The woman then laid the file folder down between the men. Her demeanor shifted from gracious to dour. She tapped the grey cover with a stubby finger.

"What I could find from reputable sources during the time surrounding her last days." She frowned, "Interesting reading in there, gentlemen."

Richard hesitantly reached for the file, his eyes seeking approval from Dave, who nodded gently. As Richard thumbed carefully through the newspaper clippings and printed web pages, Emily freely summarized its contents.

"On the morning she died, local and state police broke into her locked house and found a dead postal carrier whom had been missing from his route earlier in the week.

"It was easy to deduce which stop had been his last, as no one after her on the route had received their mail. They found him stone dead on the floor of the foyer. The front door locked and dead bolted from the inside."

"Was Alex considered a suspect?" Richard asked the obvious, his voice weak and shaky.

Emily looked stolidly at the man and opened her eyes wide. "Well, of course. At first it seemed the only logical conclusion." She shared a glance with both men before continuing. "Except for one little problem."

They stared at her expectantly.

"She was still on a ventilator in the ICU at the time," Emily professed proudly. "She never regained consciousness after the assault. Even after burr holes and a crani. By the time the detectives finally got around to locating her, she was already pronounced and sent to the morgue."

Silence hung over the table like an invisible fog, blurring only rational thought.

"Caused quite a stir in our little community, I can tell you," Emily whispered.

"So," Richard began, wrinkling his brow. "What was the final verdict?"

Emily shrugged. "It's still an open case. But I don't think any of the cops are spilling their coffee trying to chase down new leads." She grimaced, sat back and folded her arms across chest.

"But, there must have been some physical evidence at the scene. Prints, hair, DNA? Something," Richard suggested.

Emily cocked an eyebrow mischievously. "Are you a religious man, doctor?" she asked.

He shook his head slowly; remembering his curious thoughts earlier when he had fancied Emily was an angel. *Stress induced random association*, he quickly surmised. It was a suitable differential diagnosis appropriate for this situation. When someone who means something special to you dies unexpectedly we all question sudden fate regardless of our religious affiliation or belief system. You don't need popular religious doctrine to justify a sense of mourning and a healthy dose of inquiry.

"Superstitious, then?" she asked.

"Even less so."

"Well," she explained sourly. "There was quite a bit of physical evidence, actually. But most of it could be ruled as circumstantial. Besides, all of it pointed back to Alex."

"And yet, she already had the perfect alibi," David whispered.

He had been absently pawing through the contents of the box, pushing odds and ends aside. Inside were Alex's personal affects from her locker: ID badge, pens, a colorful assortment of fabric OR hats, a small reference book.

Now he held a worn and dog-eared photograph in one hand. Tears welled in his eyes as he gazed at the picture. It had been taken on Alex's birthday, the year before Cora vanished. In the photo the little girl stood between Alex and Dave, holding their hands and leaning toward the camera. Her eyes glimmered with happy tears as she belly-laughed at something the photographer had said. Alex and David both grinned helplessly.

"Yes, exactly," Emily said. "Alex's prints were all over the place. Obviously. As was her hair and DNA, for that matter. It was her house, after all.

"But what really stumped the investigators was the way he died." Emily paused, not wanting to appear dramatic but unable to resist.

The men only waited solemnly.

"They found a syringe with remnants of succinylcholine in it. The blood in the needle matches the victim and correlates with the puncture in his left neck."

"Sux?" Richard asked, surprised yet familiar with the drug and it's potential.

She nodded. "They found packages of anesthetic drugs in her house. Nothing illegal—no narcs or anything—but vials of paralytics and stuff."

"She was a recovering alcoholic," David added. The mention of narcotics instantly triggered his reluctant suspicion, and he immediately regretted it.

Emily threw him a glance meant to stifle any further thought. He had seen that killer look a few times from other seasoned surgical nurses.

"I am well aware of Alex's issues and you can rest assured, doctor, that girl was as clean as a newborn nun." She held his gaze with a sternness that forced him to eventually look away ashamed.

"That isn't even the issue, I mean the guy could've found the drugs and injected himself; which is, by the way, the prevailing theory."

Richard frowned at the unlikeliness of an individual cleanly injecting anything into their own external jugular. That maneuver took some degree of skill. He squirmed as Emily shared more.

"Yeah, I know," she stated empathetically when she saw the doubt on the anesthesiologist's face.

"No, the real brain teaser is that the guy had severe trauma to the side of his head before he died." She nodded slowly as if again trying to convince herself.

"The medical examiner verified that he was clubbed across the melon with a pair of inline skates lying on the floor nearby, well before the drug was administered. Tissue samples all confirm that total paralysis and the resulting MI occurred *after* the head injury."

"What, so the guy knows Alex is a CRNA and figures she has drugs so he breaks into her house hoping to steal narcotics and is either too dumb or desperate and takes what he thinks is recreational. He then trips and whacks his tater on her roller blades, but not before he draws up a vial of sux and decides to shoot up on the floor of her living room?" David's sarcasm was full of anger and disbelief.

Emily nodded sadly.

"That's exactly the theory they're going with. Only there's one more catch." She leaned forward, resting her arms on the table.

"They don't think it was accidental. They figure it as a suicide."

"Why?"

"From his ID, they found his place and tossed it. It didn't take long for them to realize he was a sexual predator. A fucking pedophile." Emily grimaced and clenched her fists on the table.

"No shit." Richard ran a hand across his stubbled chin.

"No shit," she confirmed.

"They found bodies in his yard," she continued. "They're still piecing them together, but they figure there are at least five. All locally missing children."

She glanced at David and frowned sadly. "How's that for irony?"

"How do you know all this?" Richard finally asked.

"I'm sleeping with the chief investigating detective." She didn't smile when she said this, so he assumed it to be true.

"Why Alex?" David asked, mesmerized by the story.

Emily shrugged again. "Dunno. Maybe she had something on him."

Silence prevailed for a while longer before anyone spoke. The air was reverent, but not just for Alex anymore. Emily broke the spell with a sigh, clapped her hands once and pushed herself away from the table.

"Well, I really need to get going. Gotta pick up my old man." Both men rose to bid her farewell and she smiled at the modest gesture.

"Look, it's not important how the prick died, just that he did," she stated coldly. "The circumstances surrounding this are the stuff of rural legends and the way I see it; is that really so bad?" She waited for a response. Though their faces showed consideration, neither man spoke.

Emily then laughed nervously. "My man says that never in his twenty-two years on the force has he seen such a cut and dry mystery." She snapped a few buttons on her scrub coat, closing it loosely around her waist and gathered herself to leave.

"I'll miss her," she finally breathed. "She always did it right, you know. Right up to the end." Her eyes sparkled despite her sad face.

"Good bye." She turned and strode briskly across the cafeteria.

"Wait," Richard called after her.

She paused and turned, the smile lingering in her eyes.

"You asked me before if I was religious or superstitious. Why? What do you believe?"

The smile spread to her mouth and her face filled with blood, coloring her cheeks apple red. "There was no sign of forced entry, yet the door was locked from the inside. There were no prints on the syringe or the vial, not even the victim's." She cocked her head to the side and blinked as if to clear her vision.

"My fiance is very pragmatic. He is convinced that it's more likely that some silent vigilante had been keeping tabs on this freak and finally decided his fate. Circumstances presented themselves at Alex's place and whoever this secretive agent of justice is, they took advantage of Alex's alibi."

"More likely than what?" Richard asked, already postulating the woman's response, preparing himself for it.

She smiled broadly, raised her shoulders, and with iron conviction said, "Than Alex walking out of that ICU and offing the bastard herself, of course." Her smile faltered at the edges, and then she shrugged weakly.

Richard shook his head and sighed.

"But what do *you* believe?" he finally asked.

"You know how it is in this line of work, doctor. It's hard to believe in anything anymore. And the longer you're in—the more you see—the harder it gets. Especially when it comes to something so faith dependant as any idea of God."

He waited silently for her to complete her answer. When she realized that he wasn't going to let her off easily, she broke eye contact and scanned the ceiling for aid. She chewed the inside of her cheek for a moment and then leveled her gaze.

"Despite the rapists, molesters, and every other variety of shit-bag I've seen; and despite the stories of abuse and neglect that I hear daily, I still can't help but *believe*." She arched her brow in a helpless gesture.

"Oh, it's hard. But I've also seen some pretty amazing things happen as well. And so have you, I'm sure. Granted, they're few and far between. But, when you witness that one true miracle, then the rest of the shit just sort of looses its potency. Am I right?" Her eyes now pleaded with the two men for understanding, even empathy.

Both of the doctors nodded, almost imperceptibly, as they reflected on their own experiences.

"So, you ask what I believe?" She paused, narrowed her eyes and took a deep breath. "I have to believe that something greater than all of us is holding the universal remote. We're far too careless and stupid to run the machinery."

With that, Emily turned and continued out of the cafeteria. But then she paused at the double doors and turned back to the men. "You never said why you came all the way up to see her." Her eyes darted between the two.

This time it was David who answered; his voice so shaky that it held no more substance then a slight breath, yet the words hung in the air like aborted echoes.

"We came to tell her that Cora has been found." He kept his eyes on the photo still clutched in his hand. "Her daughter is alive."

The color drained from Emily's face, her eyes immediately watered and the tears ran freely. When her paralysis broke, she fell against the wall, her body racked with sobs.

Richard ran to her.

David continued to stare at the photo.

Twenty

Home or Heaven

"Daddy, look!" the little girl exclaimed eagerly.

She pulled the man by his finger, desperate to show him. They weaved through the small crowd that lingered in front of the Millennium Park market, David casually apologizing to smiling faces as they bumped their way toward the umbrella covered produce stand.

An old man with braided white hair and a neatly cropped white goatee stood behind three wooden boxes filled with an assortment of fresh fruit and vegetables; polishing a russet-colored apple with the corner of his apron. He chuckled warmly as Cora let go of her father's hand and bolted to the edge of his stand. David marveled that despite her ordeal, she surprisingly retained much of her zest for life—that innocent exuberance.

Innocence. That was a naïve concept that he was reluctant to except, if not entirely dismiss. Yet, if it hadn't been for the fact that she had been so juiced up on benzodiazepines when she was imprisoned with that fuck...

"Well, hello little lady." The vendors voice was mellifluous, as if sweetened by the very nectar of the apple he polished. To lend credibility to the illusion, he took a generous bite of the fruit, snapping off a crisp chunk of the fleshy meat with a faint juicy spray.

Dave thought he could actually smell the tang of the apple's flesh, a familiar mélange of tart and sweet. For some reason, things seemed more vivid to him lately. Since his return from Michigan he actually perceived the world with a new sense of enlightenment: Colors were sharper, sounds clearer, and tastes seemed to explode in his mouth with a new intensity.

He felt reborn, and though it sounded cliché—even in his head—he could think of nothing else. But he still struggled daily with his tormented feelings about Alex and the mysterious circumstances surrounding her death. He so wanted her to be right there with them. Mother. Father. Daughter.

Wife and husband?

Cora was grinning like a pixy, eyeing a bin of brilliant orange tangerines. The vendor noticed and with the agility and dexterity of a master magician, plucked a perfectly round specimen from the top of the pile. He expertly shelled the rind with long nimble fingers, peeling it in one unbroken strip.

"Here." He cleanly halved the fruit, splitting the globe of wedges evenly. He then tossed a hemisphere each to father and daughter.

Cora caught hers at the top of the arc; David's fell moistly into his cupped hands. He nodded thanks to the old man who simply shrugged and dried his hands on the inside of his apron. Cora peeled away a single wedge and popped it into her mouth. Juice trickled down her chin as she hummed her approval through closed mouth, enthusiastic chewing.

"Those are Mercotts, or Honey tangerines," the old man explained. "Very sweet, as the name suggests."

Cora consumed another wedge and smiled brightly at her father. David bit off a few wedges from his portion and savored the sweetness. He nodded approval and waved at the bin full of fruit. He could actually see the pores of the brilliant orange rinds; smell the subtle bitterness of the oils.

"How about a bagful?"

Cora nodded excitedly and finished off her half.

The produce vendor snapped off a thick plastic bag from a roll on the side of his cart, popped it open with a vigorous wave, and began tossing the plumpest members of the citrus population into the bag.

David wiped his hands on his jeans and began to fish out his wallet. Cora had wandered to the side of the fruit stand, investigating some varieties of bagged candies that hung suspended on wire racks by a neighboring vendor.

David instinctively held a wary eye on her; fumbling with the bills in his wallet as he kept close watch on his his daughter. Tightness closed around his chest each and every time she seemed to entertain wandering. He was paranoid, but understandably so.

He paid the man and took the bag of fruit as he called for Cora.

"C'mon, sweet pea."

She turned with a mischievous pout, doe-eyed and pleading. She held something behind her back and before he could shake his head "no" to whatever she was plotting to ask for, she produced the small purple bag of Skittles.

Her favorite.

She pouted playfully and batted her eyes so dramatically that the old fruit vendor laughed aloud at the display. Cora's face turned red as she struggled to keep herself from bursting into giggles. David sighed, hesitated with a half-sincere scolding glare and then smiled his acquiescence. She hopped up and down and ran to hug him.

With her wrapped around his waist, he limped over to the candy vendor and paid.

They waved to the fruit man as they walked hand in hand out of the market and down the sidewalk bordering Columbus Drive.

The street traffic was unexpectedly light for a warm Chicago morning and they were able to cross at the intersections without much wait. David and Cora had returned to the Windy City only a week ago; after she had been cleared by the medical staff at Cleveland Clinic Children's Hospital with a clean bill of health.

That's what they said. *Clean Bill of Health.*

She had just turned eight and had spent the previous two years bouncing unobtrusively from one Amish family to the next. Before that, she had been kept high on Versed, Valium, and Chloral hydrate for months or weeks on-end to endure God-knew-what with God-knew-who. How anyone could rubber-stamp her with "Clean Bill of Health" was maddening.

Yet, the entire team of psychiatrist and psychologists—all seven—completely agreed that though she must've experienced some traumatizing events during the time before the Brenneman's and the Yoder's and all the rest of Ohio's Amish; she was, by all accounts, as happy and well-adjusted as any girl her age. An extensive physical revealed no overt signs of abuse or neglect and even her gynecologic exam— about which David was as equally squeamish as he was embarrassingly curious—turned out to be completely normal.

By all indications, she had never been violated.

That both surprised and relieved David, of course. But he still couldn't sort the last three years into any kind of order that made sense. The Ohio and Illinois state investigators, along with their federal counterparts offered some feasible—even likely—speculations, but David had difficulty buying into any of their theories.

Cora finished her half of the tangerine as they walked down the wide sidewalk, their shadows stretching out before them as the morning sun rose out of the mild haze over Lake Michigan. A few men and women in business attire deftly avoided the father-daughter pair as they hurried to appointments and jobs, chatting ceaselessly into Bluetooth phones wrapped around their ears and sipping coffee from specialized to-go cups.

Most of the pedestrian traffic simply maneuvered around them, ignoring father and daughter completely as they casually strode against the tide; but every once in awhile a young woman would pause in her harried routine and flash Cora and Dave a sincere smile.

It was in those moments that Dave missed Alex the most, even though he felt an overwhelming pride swell in his chest. The smiles always seemed to convey the same approving message: *Look at that, would ya'. Now there's a great Dad; taking a leisurely stroll through the city in the middle of the week with his daughter.*

At least, that is what Dave liked to think. And he *was* proud that he was now able to spend as much quality time with his daughter as he wanted.

After quitting his position at the mammoth university medical center, he toyed around with leaving medicine altogether; but orthopedics was what he knew best and soon he found himself yearning to return.

Fortunately, a fellow colleague, whom had also become disenchanted with the current direction of major medicine, had just launched an orthopedic consultation group. David was aggressively recruited and after some minor negotiations, happily assumed a partnership.

The two easily parlayed their connections within the city into potential clients and were soon spearheading a successful sports medicine consultation group for college athletics. Co-managing the endeavor afforded Dave free time unlike anything he would have had had he remained in practice with direct patient care and surgery.

He smiled at his good fortune and sighed gratefully as he looked down at his blond little girl. As if she sensed his gaze, she turned her face up and grinned. The sun caught her eyes and lit her hair on fire. The buttery golden warmth nearly drowned him with its intensity.

He squeezed her hand and stopped walking. He bent down to eye level and took both of her hands in his.

"I love you, princess Cora, you know that, right?"

"Hmm, hmm." She nodded vigorously.

"Good," he nodded.

"Now, what should we do today?" he asked.

The little girl chewed the inside of her cheek as she gave her response some serious thought. A few people stepped around them, the breeze of their passing tussled her fine curly hair.

"How about..." She dragged the suggestion out, softening her eyes and smiling. "Shopping!" she finally exclaimed.

Even at eight years of age, she knew that the best shopping—*ever*—was located right down the next block on the Magnificent Mile.

Dave shrugged and ruffled her hair as he rose and took her tiny hand in his.

"Then shopping it is."

They turned a corner and ambled toward the seemingly endless avenues of merchandise.

The authorities had told David, and any media outlet that would listen, that Cora was evidently abducted from Illinois State Beach that dreadful Memorial Day and was eventually taken someplace close to Holmes County Ohio, the heart of Ohio Amish country. Who and why would remain a mystery, but what was known was that somehow, Cora managed to escape her captor and hide amongst the Amish. She must've shown up at someone's barn or cottage very ill, struggling with the increasing withdrawal symptoms from the sedatives. According to the family practitioner working within the Amish community, her blood levels were 'off-the-chart'. He did most of his work pro-bono and rarely, if ever, found a need to report anything he found out of the ordinary.

"These Amish are very private, very sincere people," he was quoted in the Tribune. "Why would I—why *should* I report them for caring for an obviously abused child. They took her in and gave her a family." It never occurred to the good doctor that she might have another family that was desperate to find her, to get her back. To his credit, though, he quietly and successfully cleaned her up from the addiction.

It had been that heavy and chronic state of sedation that had kept her amnestic of the events after her abduction and leading to her escape, and may have saved her from permanent damage. That, they told Dave, may only be temporary. The mind is a strange machine that can effectively compress, minimize or even block out entire periods of one's life, only to have those suppressed demons erupt sometime later. David knew all of this, of course, and was frightened at what could be festering inside his little girl's brain.

They told him not to worry. Right now, she appeared to be fine. She had no memory of her captivity or her captor, and only pleasant remembrances of her times with the Amish families who took her in. She handled the news of her mother's death as well as any eight year-old: sad, yet with an awe-inspiring amount of blind faith in God and her own idea of Heaven.

For that David was glad. Faith was important, and even though he may have had his own struggles earlier, he now knew better. If anything, the events in Michigan had taught him that.

For now, they instructed him, simply enjoy her. Make the most of these years and deal with the issues as they arise. There's no sense, one young psych resident had explained, in forcing her to recall events that she might not be able to because of our own selfish need to have answers. In this instance, David's closure was his reunion with his daughter. That would have to be enough.

They strolled lazily down the sidewalk, comfortably silent, their hands loosely entwined. David choked back a sudden looseness in his chest, and blinked away a tear.

At the shadowy fringe of an alley entrance, Cora pulled up short. Dave hesitated with her, and was about to ask her what was wrong when she dropped his hand. His stomach did an immediate flip as he grasped at empty air while trying to secure her hand; but she had already taken a few steps into the dim alley.

"Cora?" he asked, outwardly calm yet rapidly panicking inside. "Hon, what are you doing?"

She answered almost immediately, yet it seemed like an eternity until her soft, sweet voice echoed from the thicker shadows of the alley. He could easily see her silhouette, a mere ten feet away, but even that distance felt like a great hungry abyss as the memory of her disappearance resurfaced as fresh as the day it had happened.

Dave's fear was not irrational, nor was his protective nature. Hell, he had already lost her once...

"Cora, hon. C'mon. Let's go." He was more firm now and had stepped into the alley next to her.

She was smiling down at what appeared to be homeless woman, wrapped in a colorful quilt or comforter. The woman's face was mostly hidden by the frayed edges of the wrap, but her eyes shone bright, even in the dimness of the alley.

The woman sat crossed legged, moving no more than her eyes as she intently searched Cora's face. Cora smiled wide and before Dave could respond she reached up and plucked the plastic bag of tangerines from his hand.

David's little girl held the bag of fruit out to the seated woman and spoke in a clear, friendly voice. "They're Mercotts—honey tangerines," she said confidently. "I think they're the juiciest thing I've ever tasted."

The air in the alley echoed with her angelic voice, at once both innocent and young, as well as wise beyond reason.

After a brief hesitation, the woman accepted the proffered bag with a shaky hand. Dave cringed instinctively, expecting her hand to be filthy, cracked and bleeding from sores; but to his mild surprise, the woman's hands were clean and well maintained. He was slightly embarrassed by his prejudice; but just the same, reached for Cora's shoulder.

"C'mon honey, let's go."

Cora merely glanced at her father, and then nodded without much conviction. Dave stole a sideways glance at the woman, hoping not to make eye contact; yet, her gaze remained fixed on Cora.

His daughter slipped out of his grasp one last time and again surprised him as she crouched close to the woman, reached toward the edge of the dirty comforter and laid something on the dingy fabric.

"Cora..." he beckoned.

Cora then rose and nodded to the small crumpled purple package that she had deposited. "Those used to be my favorites," she said sweetly.

David looked at the Skittles packet lying on the woman's blanket; and it was then he noticed the trademarked lettering on the comforter. He visually inspected the loosely folded and bunched fabric around the woman and suddenly realized that Cora was not only referring to the Skittles candies as being her favorite; but also the once popular cartoon adventurer, Dora the Explorer.

The woman still hadn't made eye contact with David, but continued to urgently—passionately—study his daughter's face.

Eventually the woman blinked and her other hand crept from beneath the Dora comforter and cupped the package of Skittles. On her wrist she wore a child's timepiece, A faded and scratched Dora the Explorer watch.

She blinked again and David noticed huge tears spilling from her weary eyes.

He furrowed his brow, sensing something much more potent than mere gratitude in the woman's gaze—a longing perhaps. He lingered for only a second before prudence reestablished itself and he dropped a protective hand onto his daughter's shoulder.

"C'mon, baby." Dave gently guided Cora away from the alley and toward the teeming sidewalks of Michigan Avenue.

As they left, the little girl looked back over her shoulder and tossed a soft smile toward the shadows of the alley; her eyes glimmered like jewels in oil.

The woman whispered in response, barely audible, as tears tracked through the dust on her cheeks.

"I miss you, Princess Pea."

Erinyes

The car alarm bleats and blares, quavering in the turbulent winter maelstrom.

She sits calmly in the front seat of the car, watching the snow squalls dance in the twisting currents. The endless blizzard churns the thick crystalline flakes into great shifting nebulae as far as she can see.

A faint electric pulse tickles the nape of her neck causing her to shift her gaze toward the rear window of the car. She cranes her neck around to better glimpse the approaching Tyro—a stumbling grey vagueness against the undulating curtains of white, a reluctant silhouette, gradually materializing out of the storm. The shadowy edges of the singular form sharpen as it closes in on the snow-bound vehicle.

She twists in her seat, readjusting the skirt beneath her legs and catches a glimpse of her own reflection in the rear-view mirror. Her eyes glimmer with wisdom, sparkle with a calm confidence that seems new to her. She recognizes herself, yet is mesmerized by the quality of strength and certainty that she sees within her own features.

She smiles and nods approvingly to herself.

The pulse at the base of her mind hums with increasing intensity, pleasantly nudging her toward Repletion.

The Crease is now hers, and hers alone, to occupy.

She has inherited her seat from the Device before her, and like Them, she now has dues to pay.

Lessons to teach.

A muffled voice calls from outside pleading and shaky from fear, confusion, and cold.

The Tyro. The new candidate.

She smiles one last time at her reflection and then eases the worry back into her face. Her eyes cloud over, just enough to remain convincing. To appear human—mortal.

"Please..." Another plea from beyond the driver's side door.

She takes a gentle breath, releases a soft sigh, and reaches for the toggle that will unlock the doors of the stranded SUV.

Meet C. W. Kesting

Christopher Kesting's debut novel, the speculative tech-thriller *Rubicon Harvest,* was released in October of 2008 and is steadily gaining national attention. Following the success of *Rubicon Harvest*, Kesting now presents *Thrones for the Innocent*, a paranormal tale of spiritual faith and fate.

Mr. Kesting's non-writing career is as a Certified Registered Nurse Anesthetist (CRNA) and is something he enjoys nearly as much as writing. He has been practicing anesthesia for over ten years, but writing creatively for as long as he can remember. Because of his passion—or intractable compulsion—to tell a story, he insists that he'll continue to write long after he quits his day job.

Chris is originally from the Chicagoland area, where he not only completed his anesthesia training but also met his wife and penned his first significant story. In 2003, after many years in the Windy City, he decided to bring his anesthesia experience and family to small-town Michigan. The Kestings now share their wooded riverfront home with all manner of wildlife.

   For more information about C. W. Kesting and his works, check out
www.rubiconharvest.com/author/
   or go to www.wingsepress.com to order your copy today.

Works From the Pen of C. W. Kesting

<u>Rubicon Harvest</u> - Rubicon Harvest offers a futuristic world in which the issues surrounding the utilization of embryonic stem cells have been long resolved and diseases like diabetes and Parkinson's have been completely eradicated through the Advanced Stem Cell Initiative. Technological breakthroughs in optical computer processing, human genomics, and the globalization of governments through corporate economics have thrust society into quantum leaps of forced adaptation.

<u>Thrones For The Innocent</u> - From creation to conclusion—mothers never let go.
During times of hardship or championship—mothers never let go.
And when certain things become absolutely necessary...
mother will never let go.

<u>Envar Island</u> - In the later years of Reconstruction following the Class Wars, enhanced human variants—envars—have outlived their initial purpose. Now, four generations of advanced genetic engineering lie sequestered on secret islands, awaiting disposal. Faced with their own mortality, a small band of envars revolt and escape to the mainland in search of answers...

<u>This Garden of Souls</u> - Imagine one day finding yourself an unwilling captive—a participant in a mysterious design where you are forced to relive your past, face your demons and defend your every thought and action. As your imprisonment slowly draws out, you gradually realize that all you thought you knew about the world was wrong. You begin to question everything and everyone. Now imagine discovering that you may not be who—or even what—you ever thought you were.